CLOSE

CLOSE

Bill James

This first world edition published 2017
in Great Britain and the USA by
SEVERN HOUSE PUBLISHERS LTD of
19 Cedar Road, Sutton, Surrey, England, SM2 5DA.
Trade paperback edition first published
in Great Britain and the USA 2017 by
SEVERN HOUSE PUBLISHERS LTD

British Library Cataloguing in Publication Data
A CIP catalogue record for this title is available from the British Library.

ISBN-13: 978-0-7278-8686-6 (cased)
ISBN-13: 978-1-84751-792-0 (trade paper)
ISBN-13: 978-1-78010-859-9 (e-book)

All Severn House titles are printed on acid-free paper.

Severn House Publishers support the Forest Stewardship Council™ [FSC™],
the leading international forest certification organisation.
All our titles that are printed on FSC certified paper carry the FSC logo.

Typeset by Palimpsest Book Production Ltd.,
Falkirk, Stirlingshire, Scotland.
Printed and bound in Great Britain by
TJ International, Padstow, Cornwall.

'But why always Dorothea? Was her point of view the only possible one?'

George Eliot, *Middlemarch,* Chapter 29.

ONE

Iles said, pleasantly enough, given that it was Iles, 'One of the things you'll have noticed about me, Col, is that I'm strongly aware of connections or links, in the very widest, indeed global sense, such connections, links, not always immediately obvious.'

'I don't know anyone, sir, who could come near you as to strong awareness of wide, indeed global connections or links, such connections, links, not always immediately obvious,' Harpur said with terrific sincerity.

'And so an instance before us now,' Iles replied.

'Undoubtedly, sir. But which?'

'Which what, Harpur?'

'That's certainly a point, sir.'

'What is?'

'I need specifics,' Harpur said.

'Of course you do, Col. At your rank you can't be expected to deal in general, overarching factors.'

'Thank you, sir.'

'Which specifics, Harpur?'

'This corpse hit by at least three rounds from close. It seems to me extremely specific, sir, especially to the corpse, but to us, also. In the very widest, indeed global sense, what do you see him connected to, linked to?'

'A perfectly understandable, if rough-and-ready, question, Col.'

'Thank you, sir.'

'And there is an answer, Harpur. Be assured.'

'Good.' Harpur waited for this answer. But Iles went silent for a while. They were standing near a silver Ford Focus in a cul-de-sac on the northern edge of their ground. It was a reasonably sedate area of detached and semi-detached four- or five-bedroomed houses, plus a small block of flats, near a small, well-kept park, though, obviously, the sedateness had been given quite a jolt recently. 'I certainly wouldn't want you to rush over-hastily into an explanation, sir,' Harpur said.

At once Iles replied, 'Think Billy Wilder's *Sunset Boulevard*.'

'Ah!'

'Oh, yes, Col.'

'A film?'

'You could put it like that, definitely. Think William Holden.'

'The American film star way back?'

'You could put it like that, yes,' Iles replied.

'You see a connection, a link, between William Holden and this Caucasian male, apparently executed in a Ford Focus?'

'William Holden in *Sunset Boulevard* and in the pool,' Iles said.

'Which pool?'

'We are talking about a considerable Hollywood property, with its own swimming pool.'

'I believe there are, and were, many such pools in that part of the US owing to the constant sunshine and a need to cool off.'

'California,' Iles replied.

'And William Holden is in this pool?'

'The William Holden character, Joe Gillis, face-down.'

'Not alive?'

'You could put it like that, Col. Now, you'll say to me, there's another film and a book where one of the main characters ends up dead in a luxury US property's pool, though on the other side of the USA, where there might not be so much sunshine and consequent need to cool off.'

'There's another film and a book where one of the main characters ends up in a luxury US property's pool, though on the other side of the USA, where there might not be so much sunshine and consequent need to cool off,' Harpur said.

Iles smiled very approvingly. 'You're *so* right, Col,' he said. 'Bravo! It's *The Great Gatsby*, isn't it?'

'You could put it like that, yes, sir, I think.'

'Such pools are what's known as symbolic in their various stories. But I don't want you to panic at a rather unusual word, "symbolic". To you these bathing pools might appear to be simply bathing pools. But that is in the nature of symbols, Col. They have their ordinary existence – what we might call their bathing pool, hole-in-the-ground, water-filled existence – but also they represent something of much larger significance. They indicate that wealth has its dark, dangerous side as well as its enjoyable aspect. Normally in these pools someone with a glass of Tia Maria in one hand would be floating, luxuriating, on an inflatable mattress, probably bright and cheerful in colour, the water brilliantly clean and glistening. Occasionally, though, there comes a marked change of tone and of personnel. We get a message, don't we, Col, you as a detective chief superintendent, I as an assistant chief constable (operations)? These pools and their unusual contents speak to us and to readers and audiences generally.'

'But Ford Focus man is not in a pool, sir, he's in a modest car, its front-side windows shattered. Yet you still see connections, links – connections, links to both pools?'

'The deployment of the pools in those two tales is not the same, though, is it, Col?'

'Deployment?'

'Ask yourself, Col, where does the pool actually come in each of those stories.'

'Where does the pool actually come in each of those stories?'

'Sharp, Col. Very sharp. You've put your finger on it,' the ACC said.

'I'm glad. As I see things, sir, that's my main role.'

'What is, Col?'

'To put my finger on it, whatever it is.'

'We are surely bound to notice, aren't we, Harpur, that in *The Great Gatsby*, Gatsby is found dead in his pool and this comes near the end of the book or film, so we know about the series of events and errors leading to this situation? He doesn't have to explain. We have followed the narrative.'

'He can't explain, can he, sir, because he's dead?'

'Whereas, Gillis, the William Holden figure in *Sunset Boulevard*, although dead from the very beginning, is going to be the voice that takes us through all the incidents and tensions moving forward to, or rather, moving back to, his appearance dead in the water, as the phrase goes, literally in this case. This dead man actually creates the tale, Harpur.'

'When you said, "Think *Sunset Boulevard*, think William Holden" this was what you meant, was it, sir?'

'Excellent, Col.'

'You see a connection, a link, owing to the very great, indeed, global, width of your vision when dealing with connections and links, such connections and links not always immediately obvious?'

'Exactly, Col.'

'You believe that this cadaver here, although not in a pool, will, when we look at his history in exceptional depth, tell us how he happens to be discovered with parts of his face and forehead carried away by what must have been bullets of some substantial calibre.'

'That's what I was getting at, Col – the connection, the link, to a notable precedent, viz, William Holden. And that's what I was getting at when I spoke of width and fixed on the term "global". My mind will range and explore, seeking these connections and links. It's a brilliantly positive, unflagging restlessness. I'm not one to be tethered, Harpur.'

'I've heard people say you are the least tethered person they have ever come across, putting them in mind of an unbroken-in mustang, proud, free, dangerous, its muzzle spit-flecked.'

'If the world is out there, Col – and out there is where it undeniably is or where else, for God's sake? – one must trek through it, take from it willy-nilly, conjoin its many outpourings and modes. To neglect such opportunities is a kind of dereliction, a kind of unforgivable indolence.'

'But, surely, sir, this is routine. Whenever we come across a murdered male or female, the priority is to discover her/his history and background. He/she can't help us, because she/he's dead. This one's the same.'

'Joe Gillis helped. More: he told the whole lot to us, the audience, Harpur, and the cameras took his dictation. You'll have heard of that chant that goes up in some American jails when a prisoner is being escorted to the electric chair.'

'"Dead man walking"?'

'Good, Col. Here, though, we have dead man *talking*. If you Google you'll find that quite a few writers have used this amended version as the title for their books and/or films if the yarn is being told by someone no longer alive.'

'The man in the car is not Joe Gillis, though, is he? Well,

obviously, there's no actual Joe Gillis. He's a figment, sir, created by scriptwriters. But the man in the Focus we know to be Thomas Wells Hart, early twenties, a private investigator on our ground and real. I've met him occasionally when he was investigating some case that interested us, as well.'

'Chandler's private eye, Philip Marlowe, was always running into local cops and making them look stupid,' Iles said. 'But that doesn't necessarily mean the same for you, Col. You don't need such help.'

'Thank you, sir. And there were those anon letters about him that came to us alleging under-age sex. They turned out to be wrong because he wasn't.'

'Wasn't what?'

'Under-age. The letters claimed he was the victim – had been seduced as a schoolboy by a teacher.'

Iles paused for a second. He would jab his astonishing memory into performance. He said, 'The teacher female? Do I get her name right – Judith Vasonne?'

'She moved away.'

'I don't think we ever identified anon, did we, Col?'

Harpur said . . .

TWO

But why always Harpur? Was his point of view the only possible one? What would Ford Focus man say if he ran this tale?

THREE

You'll possibly expect something wry and vain from me about the indignity of being found shot dead in such an ordinary car as a Ford Focus, and in an unspectacular suburban street, unspectacular because it's a cul-de-sac going nowhere and going there after only the frontage width of eight detached and semi-detached houses, numbers 1 to 15 on the north side and 2 to 16 on the south, plus a minor block of flats. This is certainly not the death situation I would have chosen. But it's hard to imagine a situation I *would* have chosen.

The location is not really the important factor here. The important factor, or factors, is/are the three bullets now at rest inside me, two in the face-head area, one in the upper chest, missing the heart, though not by much, and, in any case, virtually redundant because each skull and brain injury could have killed. My impression is of soft-nosed dumdum rounds designed to spread and splinter on major impact causing extensive internal damage to the target. And, because of the loss of penetrative sleekness when it broadens like that, liable to stay spent in the hit body and not speed hungrily through it, and out again, perhaps endangering others. People who sweepingly condemn dumdums as barbaric usually do so without realizing there is this beneficial, humane side to their use. Salvoes and that kind of thing can be dangerous not just for the person they're aimed at, but for anyone in the immediate area. Reduction of that peril is clearly a plus, though, in view of what's happened many folk might find it odd that I should plead for a more balanced view of dumdums.

Also, there is, in fact, quite a lot to be said in favour of the Ford Focus for my type of work. I'm slightly reluctant to refer to myself as a 'private investigator'. To me this is an American term covering characters like Raymond Chandler's Philip Marlowe, a great guy, but a great guy at a distant time and at a distant place – Bay City (actually, Santa Monica), California. Yet a private investigator is what I am, was. This is why I say the

Ford Focus seemed just right for my professional needs and therefore, of course, appropriate for me to get shot in if I'm going to get shot at all. Suppose Raymond Chandler's Marlowe had ended up killed in his car, it would most probably have been the equivalent type of inconspicuous vehicle – though not actually a Ford Focus because they weren't around then in Bay City – or Britain.

But it's the 'inconspicuous' element that is crucial, here or in the US. Some refer to the Ford Focus as a 'teacher's car', and it's true you'll see plenty of them parked in school yards. I'll admit it's a rather patronizing description, meaning a car bought mainly for getting to and from work, affordable out of a limited salary, unpretentious and so not liable to get its wheel nuts loosened by jokey pupils. The Focus is, and was during my time as a detective, a fine, stolid model. It didn't stand out, wasn't especially noticeable, despite its title, Focus, seeming to demand close examination. And, obviously, these qualities made it very suitable for tailing and for covert surveillance; and for moving a client, or clients, secretly to a different, possibly safer base. A private investigator would be unwise to run a Porsche or Maserati. Unwise for two reasons: extreme, inconvenient notability; extravagance – clients might feel they were buying the investigator a very high life.

No, the Ford Focus and a couple of other similar motors were ideal for my occupation, but could not offer total, perfect invisibility and protection, obviously.

FOUR

I sort of drifted into this game. I can't say I drifted out of it, though. That had an abrupt, point-blank, finale nature. To be fair, it was, in fact, a very tidily organized bit of onslaughting, every possibility of mistake (theirs) or escape (mine) cut to the minimum. Obviously, their first and chief success was – unknown to them – my belief I'd find something satisfactory at number 12B Cairn Close. Something necessary? This meant big help, maybe conclusive help, with the hellishly tricky corruption investigation I'd been floundering about in for months.

Of course, I knew who had asked me as a favour to do a quick check on Cairn Close: a friendly, very temporary colleague who'd been working with me on that formidable investigation I've just spoken of. We'd thought we were closing in on major truths, and some major people. These major people would not have carried out the killing personally, though. This formal duty could have been farmed out to jobbers impressively experienced in seeing off some nominated target or targets in a suburban cul-de-sac. It would be a fairly rare and therefore expensive kind of skill to hire; but possibly regarded as justified if the commission were nicely carried out with no pointers to the ultimate originator, originators, of the gun-play. There might be suspicion, intelligent, logical suspicion, but suspicion only: plenty of that around always, though most of it never came to anything.

I'm ashamed – a bit too late – of letting myself get sat-navved into what I knew was a close. Some stupidity! Some lapse of vigilance! I wouldn't say that was typical of me. Suicidal of me? More like it. Cairn was a narrow-mouthed close, capable of letting in from or letting out to Joel Street, the main drag, one car at a time. It culminated in a little circular area around which the higher-numbered houses stood. I think I'd already sensed it was disastrous, naïve foolishness for me to take the Focus into this noose, even before I heard the vehicle behind. I was supposed to be an expert on tailing techniques, but there might be even better ones around. Perhaps I'd grown smug and over-confident. Maybe I was only good at being the tail, not at realizing when I had a tail myself – in fact, two tails. The first followed me into Cairn Close, I looked in the mirror and saw a Mazda 6 saloon immediately behind me, and behind the Mazda some sort of estate car had pulled across the entrance to Cairn so there would be no entrances or exits for, say, a minute; vehicle as moveable barrier, a trick possibly learned from *The Godfather 1* film.

I stopped as soon as I felt something might be wrong, which was probably another bit of lame-brain. It gave them – the occupants of the Mazda – a stationary, easy to hit, objective: me, immobile behind the wheel, my head and upper chest encouragingly framed by the door window. The 'them' – the cul-de-sac artists – would be two, possibly three. Blasts came from both sides, plus a lot of glass splinters, the heavier barrage from the right. This would figure, because they'd know I'd be in the driving perch on that side, but it's difficult to be precise in such a het-up, terminal situation.

It's interesting to recall that Captain Scott was buried under a cairn near the South Pole.

FIVE

In her own, rather roundabout and flamboyant way, Judith Vasonne, the sweetly built Careers teacher at school, was very influential in setting me off in the private investigator profession. She had real, true insight, as well as all the rest of it. When I went to see her during my last year in the sixth form it didn't really mean very much. I was thinking of trying for a place at university and only went to consult Judy because she looked the way she did, and because she might know of some recruitment openings which were so brilliantly attractive that I'd forget about university and the fees burden and get out there and start earning pay and promotion.

In fact, Judith had recommended a college course in chiropody, which she gleefully pointed out could lead either to a post in the National Health Service or in a private practice, with the possibility of an eventual partnership and even to the establishment of my own foot business.

Careers was only one section of her work. She taught Religious Studies.

Apparently as a chiropody selling-point she'd said, 'There'll always be feet, Tom. You'll remember *Isaiah:* "How beautiful upon the mountains are the feet of him that bringeth good tidings, that publisheth peace." The mountains are not crucial to this thought, and it's a flagrant *non-sequitur* to think that because the feet are upon a mountain they will be beautiful. Some feet are ugly and no amount of mountaineering will make them beautiful. This is the chiropodist's function and his/her consulting room will be just as effective at sea level as on the Eiger. Yes, there'll always be feet, and there'll always be *trouble* with feet – in-growing toenails, fallen arches, corns, gout, bunions, callused soles, deformities from cruelly high heels. There is opportunity in feet. 'The logic and thoroughness of this topic, backed up by the Old Testament, had seemed powerful, irresistible. Isaiah had always struck me as a prophet you shouldn't short-change. I felt

half trapped by her glowing patter. I wanted to run from her –
take the good tidings and peace to somewhere else, not necessarily
mountains. As a matter of fact, my feet were OK and would have
got me away fast. But out of politeness, and because she had
encouraging breasts, today under a sketchy mauve bra and insub-
stantial silk blouse, I stayed a while, did some good nodding
bordering on keenness, asked a few intelligent chiropody-type
questions, such as the growth rate of toenails at the differing
ages of a patient, and took a stack of literature from her: employ-
ment pamphlets and brochures, not the Old Testament.

I was shuffling with showy vim through this lot, my face, I'm
pretty sure, bright with interest, when she grabbed it all back
from me with her long, varnish-free, elegant fingers, plainly
custom-made for pouncing, and flung it up in the air, like an
explosion in a magazines and journals store.

She said, 'This bores you speechless, doesn't it?'

'Not speechless. Just bores me, scares me.'

'Good. I wouldn't want to think of you as thrilled by foot
care.'

'I don't understand. It's part of your job, isn't it?'

'What?'

'To guide us towards satisfying, secure work, regardless of the
undeniable *non sequitur*, "How beautiful upon the mountains,".'

'Stuff *Isaiah*,' she replied.

I was still only a teenager but I felt the tone of things between
us had begun to change.

SIX

So, the feet bumf flew and floated and nose-dived. It takes quite an effort to regard this quaint episode as the start of something darkly serious; and more than darkly serious for me, pardon the personal moment.

I want to speculate a little further about the programme of events in Cairn Close that night. Consider the estate car, their moveable bulwark, immediately placed across the entrance-exit once I'd committed the Focus to Cairn, followed by the Mazda. It was a sophisticated touch, wasn't it? It wasn't there to stop me getting out. I'd have had to turn the Ford Focus and knock the Mazda out of the way first. No, the estate car's main task was to prevent any other vehicle getting in − *say* someone returning home or simply visiting. It seemed to me a procedure the driver had swiftly improvised: one car enters to carry out the mission, the other to ensure there were no accidental interruptions. These people were flexible quick thinkers.

So the Focus would have to sit there and take whatever came, and what came was sure to come very capably. Then the estate car would move away, allowing the Mazda to back out, and both vehicles could exit the area at a legal speed so as to remain unnoticeable by any police vehicle or some public spirited pest with a mobile phone.

In Cairn there must have been at least two sharpshooters. Both Focus front side windows were smashed. As we've seen, because the bullets were almost certainly dumdum they would lodge at the first substantial point of contact, e.g. a flesh-and-bone body. They wouldn't pass through it, possibly breaking, say, the left window, already having smashed the right at the onset, or vice-versa. Two shattered windows meant two weapons minimum.

Clearly, these gunmen knew their trade well. In this kind of operation − blitzing a car from opposite points − there would be a danger that if one or both missed the target the colleague, colleagues, on the other side would get hit by friendly fire, whether the bullets were dumdum or not. An absolute miss, or more than one absolute miss, would mean that the bullet, bullets, of whatever type, had found nowhere to nestle until it, they, got to the mate, mates, over there, left or right. The attack party must have been very sure they would make a neat job of it, and that rounds with my name and price on them would go to the correct destination: upper-body me.

I wondered whether they did any checks to make sure I was dead. I could have assured them on this, but, of course, the dead don't declare themselves dead; it would be self-obsession. Handguns, even when used by high quality marksmen, are not always totally accurate: they kick, they veer. Those two or more would be able to see I'd certainly taken hits, but not that I'd taken hits in exactly the right spot or spots to end life. I refer to *The Godfather* again: Don Corleone gets struck by five close-range pistol rounds from the Turk's gang while buying fruit at a stall but still survives until halfway through the film and a massive, natural causes, flowers-aplenty, crook funeral.

The contingent in Cairn would probably feel reluctant to open a car door and get close enough to do a pulse test. It would slow down their getaway. There'd be blood everywhere inside the Focus. Permit another film mention, please: remember that scene in *Pulp Fiction* where a car passenger is accidentally shot causing a terrific, inconvenient mess. The Cairn team would want to make sure they didn't get mucked up by my blood and fragments, wouldn't they? This wasn't squeamishness or insult but a basic, sensible precaution. I can sympathize with that attitude. Blood is all very admirable when carrying out its true, useful function, freighting oxygen around the physical frame, including, of course, the happy production of stiffies in males. But spattered and on the loose it's an entirely different commodity. I'll vouch for that.

And yet, if these were people hired to do a killing for a good fee, half in advance, half on completion, and managed only something less than a killing, mere woundings and/or disablements, they wouldn't qualify for the full payment, so it was possible they did satisfy themselves I was an indisputable goner. They'd certainly get no argument from me in this regard. Death has its own decorum, or should.

Before setting out on this trip to 12B Cairn Close I'd naturally checked via the electoral register and so on who lived thereabouts. Immediate neighbours included a couple called Nape – Felix and Veronica, not people known to me or to any of my usual sources. Maybe Bait would have been a more suitable name, though they probably wouldn't realize why.

'Felix, there's a fucking Ford Focus getting shot up in the close, love.'

'Really, darling?'

SEVEN

S o, yes, the feet bumf had flown and floated and nose-dived. This was a significant sixth-form day, a day to shape, re-shape lives, Judith Vasonne's as well as mine. I don't think it's an exaggeration to say the situation had one or two unusual aspects. After all, it featured a religious education teacher contemptuously flinging everywhere very well-meant, illustrated career guidance booklets about toes and feet generally and, in the same couple of moments, bellowing, 'Stuff *Isaiah*,' her voice likely to carry to other class rooms in this ersatz, breeze-block building, and even as far as the headmaster's study. He might not care one way or the other about *Isaiah,* but most likely he would find her din inappropriate. And 'inappropriate' in that kind of world meant fucking outrageous.

Would it be wrong to say a kind of alliance, even a kind of intimacy, between us had been built by this behaviour? Would she have allowed herself to show such disregard for honest chiropody material and for the scriptures in front of anyone else? True, some others might have heard her brash *Isaiah* put-down through these flimsy walls, but that was only part of the performance. The full unscholastic show had been reserved for me, her chosen audience, hadn't it, right up there at epiphany standard? That's how I saw things at the time and, of course, subsequently.

She obviously thought she was only bringing into open view what I really felt about a future in feet, but was too timid and/ or polite to disclose. My prophet quote – choked off by her – Judith would probably regard as a ruse to charm and flatter by parading something I'd just learned from her. True, we were still teacher and pupil, but this couldn't be the complete picture any longer, surely. My guess was she disliked the isolation of her job. She looked for someone who could help her escape now and again and picked me. I didn't mind this one bit.

She'd be about twenty-two or three. I was seventeen. Perhaps she'd deliberately shortened the small age difference by acting like a steamed-up kid – making paper planes of the brochures, yelling her silly, disrespectful snarl at *Isaiah*. There are more than sixty chapters in that book: a lot to stuff. And to stuff *Isaiah* is to stuff also Handel's oratorio, *The Messiah*, which is largely based on it, especially the start.

It made me feel quite adult to analyze her behaviour like this, unscramble her motives and aims. Roles reversed? But maybe she had counted on that. It might be a two-pronged ploy. What do I mean by this? It's complicated, but possible just the same: did Judy want to make herself seem younger by her infantile, wild carry-on, and, contrariwise, did she want to make me seem older by giving me the chance cleverly to spot why she wanted to seem younger? Convergence. This is the reason I said she put me on the way to the investigator career, and ultimately to Cairn Close closure, though I would never blame her for that – supposing I was in a position to blame anyone. As Andrew Marvell, a poet I studied at A-level, almost said, 'The grave's a fine and private place/But none, I think, do there retrace/The hows and whys that put them there.'

Judith had a one-bedroom, second-floor flat quite sanely decorated in a private block a couple of miles from the school, and an old red Honda saloon given her by her father, so we were able to meet without much trouble. She wanted us to be what she called 'sensibly discreet'. It seemed a weird phrase to come from someone who could get so noisily haywire. But I thought I understood the change.

Affairs between teachers and pupils were not generally approved of even when the pupil was over the age of consent such as me then. Teachers could get sacked and blacklisted for that kind of saucy liaison. The censure was probably stronger when the affair involved a female teacher and a male pupil rather than a male teacher and a girl pupil. This arose from a kind of compliment to women. It assumed them to be steadier, more controlled, less lustful than men. The shock hit harder when one of them junked this decorous recipe. Judy said we should be as careful as we could be. I agreed with this. Most probably my parents wouldn't think it nice for me to be having it off with a school mistress three times a week, and occasionally four or five, especially when the school mistress's special area of interest other than their son was the holy Bible. They'd think chaos loomed. And, another reason for caution: Judy had an older brother and sister-in-law living in what I gathered was a big place just outside the city, towards Rastelle Major, She probably wouldn't want them to know about her special kind of love life.

Judith mentioned a novel, adapted as a film, called *An Untimely Romance,* by someone named D.B. Nailsea, dealing with this kind of education-based sexual hotchpotch and trying to portray sensitively the emotions involved. Judith did seem set on a romance and if there were people who knew of it or suspected it they would probably agree with the reproach in that book's title, 'untimely'. In fact, some might find this a bit mild. The school had several rancid old cows on the staff who might want to expose and punish Judith, so I made myself watchful when on my way to and from her flat, or when she drove me back to near my parents' house in Gowter Avenue after a jaunt. She said she'd always hated the Honda because of its lines and garish colour, but now she'd become fond of it, grateful for it and to it. She mentioned an editor of the *New Yorker* magazine who struggled to keep all traces of smut out of its pages but failed to see the suggestiveness in a cartoon that showed a couple leaving their parked car and walking towards some dense woodland, the man carrying the vehicle's back seat. Judith did a lot of reading and could refer to all sorts. So, we could both make references. I enjoyed this. It meant we had more together than just sex.

My vigilance around the two locations paid off. During several days I began to notice a recurring figure, sometimes near Judith's place and sometimes near where I lived. This was a slight, nimble-looking, middle-height Caucasian man, usually in a black anorak worn open over a dark blue T-shirt, jeans, suede boots, woollen bobble hat. He'd be about twenty-three or four. Most people know from TV drama about the techniques of secret surveillance and tailing. One of the tricks is never to meet the target's eyes. This character never met mine. But I sensed that when I wasn't watching him he'd be watching me.

From Judy's flat to where I, my parents and brother and sisters, lived was about a mile and a half, walkable, most of it through busy streets full of multi-cultured shops and restaurants. This geography made the surveillance quite easy. There were plenty of people about all day and well into the evenings. He wouldn't stand out as he might have if trying to shadow me on an empty stretch of pavement. He could pretend to do some occasional window shopping, to pass the time. In extreme crisis – that is, if he feared he might have been spotted – he could even go into one of the shops briefly, or take a couple of minutes in the foyer of Moviemad, a multi-screen cinema.

I think it must have been the consistency day-by-day of his clothes that made me fix attention on him. Ironic this. Most probably he'd done what the snoop's training manual laid down as mandatory and adopted such a dark, anti-flamboyant outfit so as to merge easily with other pedestrians, and remain more or less entirely anonymous. But eventually this attempt to stay unnoticed grew noticeable because of the flagrant effort to be unnoticed.

Perhaps I failed to pick him out on the first couple of times he did one of his lurks. He and his dreary gear must have been unintentionally recorded in my waste-not-want-not subconscious, though. Repetition piled up these inadvertent memories until my sluggish workaday mind began to get nudged into awareness of them. And then the self-effacing garb became the opposite. I asked myself why was he so continually there, apparently without a change of clothes?

I didn't get an answer immediately. It took me a while to connect this dogged, drab-looking spy with Judy's dread of a spiteful, malign colleague. Had one of the school staff, driven by jealousy, envy, moral primness, hired a professional nose to fashion a case against her? It wasn't just his uniform that made him seem experienced in this kind of work. There was the eye-contact avoidance. There was the scrupulously preserved distance between him and me: generally about twenty-five metres, and swiftly readjusted to that after a temporary forced change. There was, too, the occasional use of a mobile phone, as if he were cooperating with another gumshoe – though I couldn't see one – or perhaps with a controller in an office somewhere.

Those TV crime and spy plays often demonstrated not just surveillance skills, but tricks the tracked person could use to deal with those skills, dodge out of them, confound them, counter them, negate them. The aim then was to reverse the situation. By this I mean suddenly, somehow, change pace and direction and find some cover that takes the quarry out of the stalker's sight. Disappear. This is stage one of the ploy. The next, more important and difficult manoeuvre is to get craftily behind the tail and become one yourself, transform him/her into the quarry her or him self: find where she/he comes from and who sent him/her.

This I managed to do. I found I had a flair for tag-along, street-level stealth. It thrilled me. It killed me.

EIGHT

'Despite the damage to his face, Col, you're confident about your identification of him?'

'Oh, certainly, sir,' Harpur said. 'He belongs, belonged to the . . .'

But why always Harpur and Iles?

NINE

Consider supermarkets. There was one on the route between Judith's flat and my parents' house. I had a thought: weren't they the nearest thing to a maze possible in the middle of a city? The comparison nudged me one day as I was walking to Judy's flat with the tail at a varying twenty-five metres behind, but not varying very much from that twenty-five metres. Later on, when I had moved fully into private investigating as my career, preferred to feet, I discovered that in this profession the use of supermarkets for ditching a tail was widely acknowledged and practised; pretty well a trade cliché. Some argued that Tesco was a reverse acronym meaning 'Out-class Subtly Every Tail,' and Asda a straight acronym for 'Act Swiftly to Ditch any Accompaniment'. Supermarkets, in fact, come a very respectable second to tube stations as most convenient for shedding a pest; remember that crook in one of the *French Connection* films evading the cop by some clever antics at a tube train door and waving an infuriating goodbye as it moves off with him safely aboard and the pursuit helpless on the platform?

Yes, the supermarket tactic is a good, basic stand-by. And although it's not always and totally a success, I couldn't see any faults with it when I made my off-the-top-of-the-head decision that day to try a shake-off in this big store. I'd learn about the potential snags later. I'd learn a lot of things later, but a lot wouldn't be enough, or I wouldn't now be the late Thomas Wells Hart.

One dangerous point about a supermarket not obvious to a novice is that CCTV will almost certainly fix on you, scuttling about between sections, clearly very alert and watchful, but not alert and watchful about things to buy. Supermarkets offer things to buy – it's why they exist. So, if someone doesn't buy, questions will be asked. Those monitoring the screens somewhere will wonder why she/he is there and they'll keep the focus on him/her to find out. Of course, it would be mad for someone trying to escape surveillance to make a purchase or purchases, requiring next a very public display at the checkout; perhaps a very long public display in a queue. The supermarket is supposed to offer obscurity, not a static, blatant presentation. If the hunter had lost you because you skipped about cleverly between the various aisles, she/he will definitely find you now.

And if, in order to look like a normal shopper, you did choose some items and then try to escape without paying, security at the door would most probably stop you; more unwanted public display. Security would have been earpiece-warned by the CCTV crew to look out for this dubious customer. And you might be just as likely to get stopped if you'd selected nothing. Why were you in the shop at all, in that case?

With supermarkets, it's the multiplicity of separate aisles blanked off from one another which can be so splendidly helpful, isn't it – the maze element I mentioned? If you're in, say, 'Frozen Meats' you can't tell who's over there with the 'Cereals, Biscuits and Dips' even though the two parallel shelf systems might be immediately adjacent, only a couple of feet apart.

A wise and experienced tail will know the problems certain to face him/her if she/he follows the target into the store and its aisles between shelved walls. Accordingly, he/she might choose to remain outside; there's only one exit and the operation can be resumed when she/he reappears. But not all tails are so flexible. They've been rigorously trained to keep the twenty-five metre rule and can't free themselves from it, can't adapt, can't face the risk. They have to try to stick robotically with the objective. They wouldn't know the meaning of that Latin phrase, *ad hoc* – action exclusively for one particular occasion.

And even if they did know it they would be unable and/or unwilling to apply it. As a result, the in-store tail can be considerably less than twenty-five metres from the quarry but, without a bird's-eye view, can't see her/him because of, say, the 'Boil In The Bag Kippers And Smoked Mackerel' shelves or 'Domestic Hygiene'.

On that day, I seemed to be lucky. I didn't buy anything, but put on a bit of frustrated head-shaking in front of the DVD shelf, as though angry they didn't have what I wanted. I was able to walk out unchallenged into the car park while the tail was still in 'Soft Drinks and Mixers'. To the immediate left of the entrance was a 'While You Shop' car wash, an open square area of ground where the vehicles could be hosed and polished. At the back and on one side of this square stood ten-feet-high brick walls. I found I could stand outside the cleaning area, behind the corner they formed, and watch the store's entrance while more or less hidden. Walls had become a bit of a theme in that day's events.

After about ten minutes, the tail appeared. He stood in the doorway systematically eyeballing the whole car park. I pulled back a few more inches but could still keep observation. Although totally new to this game I realized that the next phase would be the most difficult, and potentially the most revealing. I had to hope he'd give up, admit to himself that he'd lost me, and go back to wherever he'd come from. I'd try to follow him then. But the failure would make him very tense and very aware of the people around him and sticking with him. Me. I'd have to risk this, though. If there were a plot against Judy, we needed to get the details of it. I had to act with a slice of responsibility, prove myself adult, not a kid who could be scared off; or who was too lazy and indecisive to go on with this chance.

A blue Twingo Renault saloon entered the car park, flashed its headlights and found a space near Darkclad. At once a squat, middle-aged man in jeans and an unduly long beige lightweight jacket left the car and waddled fast towards the tail. They talked briefly. Twingo-man seemed ratty, flinging his short arms about, maybe to signal astonishment; not good astonishment, probably amazement that Darkclad could lose me. I guessed he must have mobiled Twingo to tell him the situation and perhaps to ask for help. Twingo might be his boss. They turned and went back into the store, Twingo presumably convinced I must still be in there.

The arrival of this car seriously changed prospects. Eventually those two would have to concede that I'd somehow sneaked out of the store. Darkclad probably believed it already. How else could he go on missing me inside – that's how he would think.

Then, they would almost certainly leave in the car. I couldn't follow. If I'd had an expense account I might have been able to call a taxi and ask the driver to wait and then dog the Twingo. But taxi drivers probably wouldn't care for that kind of possibly hazardous caper. And, I didn't have an expense account, nor a pocket full of cash.

I wondered whether the Twingo might be important in another way, though. It was about 50 metres from me, so I thought that, while they were still in the store, I'd slip over and hope there was something on view through the windows that might give useful information – documents or packages with an office address on them, for instance. I think I knew this was unlikely but what else could I try? I might be able to get an identification from the registration number, but that required illegal, bribed cooperation by someone at the Driver and Vehicle Licensing authority or the police computer. Not in my range.

I left my spot at the washery and walked at an unremarkable, ordinary pace to the Twingo. I did a swift gaze in at the dashboard shelf and the front and rear seats. There was nothing but a CD box of Henry James's *The Bostonians.*

'Do you like James, Thomas?' a gentle voice said behind me, possibly a West Country burred accent. 'Too wordy and convoluted for you, perhaps.' I turned and found both of them there, the older, podgier one smiling with extreme matiness.

The shock made me speechless for a second or two and then I said, 'I wanted to have a look at the fittings of a Twingo. I haven't seen many of them about.'

'Some have a notice on the back window, "My other car is an identical Twingo". I gather you did very well at agile slipperiness in the store, Tom,' he said. 'Good evasivenesss. It seemed to me that someone with those kinds of abilities wouldn't give up – wouldn't be satisfied with mere dodging. You'd hang about, recognizing an opportunity. Car contents might be part of that opportunity. It's why I shammed re-entry to the store. We needed to watch the car, didn't we? Rory here had bungled things, they had to be corrected. He's naturally ashamed of his uselessness. We could do with a lad like you on our staff. I know there are attractions at the school – or one major attraction, possibly – but isn't it time to enter the grown-up work world?'

'I'm due to try for Cambridge.'

'Rory went to Cambridge. Came away with a first in anthropology. Did it do anything for him in a fucking supermarket crisis, though?'

I wondered if Twingo wore that over-long jacket to make himself appear quaint and out of touch. He wasn't.

TEN

Of course, Harpur remembered . . .
But why sometimes Harpur?
Why? Because in certain ways this Ford Focus death
echoed two previous killings. There might be handy pointers in
the resemblances – and in the non-resemblances. This is a tale
that will skip about a little as far as time is concerned. It was
the sight of Iles staring into the Ford through the smashed driver's-
side window that sent Harpur's mind back to those earlier deaths:
a Jaguar, then, though,[1] and Iles had been at its near-side window.

Images from those days had stuck with Harpur: Iles, uniformed,
though capless, had been standing on the opposite side of the
Jag from him, the assistant chief's head and face framed in the
window space as he examined the interior of that car. Iles had
seen, as Harpur also had, a woman and her young stepson dead
from bullet wounds, her stepdaughter blood-drenched but alive
alongside her dead brother in the back.

Now, Harpur and Iles, uniformed but capless, stood on each
side of the Focus looking in almost as they had with the Jaguar,
but at a man shot dead behind the wheel, his visible wounds
wide and messy, maybe dumdum done from very close in the
close. No passengers.

Such an appalling mistake, those Jaguar murders. As revealed
later, a contract specialist had been hired to knock off Manse
Shale, one of the city's two most celebrated, blue-chip drugs
dealers, who would normally have been driving the children to
their private school. On that morning though, he was at a business meeting elsewhere and his wife, his second wife, took over
the duty, and she and the children were ambushed at a road
junction. The gunman had obviously panicked. He'd been
commissioned to hit a Jaguar at this spot and at a predictable
time, so he *had* hit a Jaguar at this spot and at a predictable time,

[1] See *I Am Gold*

without bothering to identify the driver, or even get the gender right; and without, either, guarding against collateral damage to the boy.

What Harpur saw now, and what he knew Iles would see, was the basic similarity – car murders by gun shots – but also basic differences. The attack on the Jaguar had been a nicely planned but dismally executed daylight operation: a badly picked, possibly junkie and/or alco, hitman not properly master of himself or his handgun; a named location where at that a.m. time there could be all sorts of traffic complications, delays and obstructions, possibly causing rushed, blaze a-fucking-way action from the visitor; an apparent failure by those who sent him to foresee a possible change in the school-run driver and to order postponement or cancellation of the gunnery in that case.

But for the Cairn Close night operation Harpur had the feeling that there had probably been no planning, only brilliant, ruthless adaptability. He would not have been able to say why he believed this, though: an instinct, and occasionally his instincts were sound. When the shooting started the Control Room took three 999 alarm calls from people living in the close, and they'd all mentioned a Mazda behind a Focus and a black estate car placed across the entrance/exit, trapping the Focus in the cul-de-sac, blocked front by the dead end and back by two vehicles. Harpur's impression was that the whole incident lasted only a couple of minutes, and then a fast withdrawal of the estate car allowing the Mazda to reverse out. Both vehicles vamoosed.

Iles, speaking across the body from the driver's-side wrecked window to Harpur at the passenger-side wrecked window, said, 'Hart. Do I get that right, Col?'

'Thomas Wells Hart.'

'Working for the Righton Private Inquiries firm under Bainbridge Williamson?'

'Promoted to a partnership lately. He was doing well. He'd be still under thirty.'

'Doing *too* well?'

'We come across him occasionally – the Stave operation and Lodestar.'

'Yes, now I recognize him. Do either of those explain why he drives into a dead-end?'

'We'll have to do some door knocking, sir.'

'Wake Thomas Wells Hart with thy knocking. I would thou coulds't, Col.'

'That I cant'st, sir, but we'll do the knocking anyway.'

'In his game he should know the perils, shouldn't he, and ought to live by that supreme piece of wisdom: "cherish your exit".'

'Maybe he thought he was OK. But then the Mazda turns up.'

'That's what I mean, Harpur.'

'What, sir?'

'He's not a novice is he?'

'Been at it for years. He started young. Straight from school.'

'So, he should have catered for the Mazda or something like it to turn up.'

'He must have thought nobody knew he'd go to Cairn Close. Confidential business.'

'That's the second rule in our and his trade, isn't it, Col?'

'What, sir?'

'If you have extremely secret and confidential material, always assume that someone else has it, too, in this case the Mazda gun party.' Iles didn't move away from the ex-window but continued inspecting Thomas Hart, the body tilted forward slightly to the right of the wheel. 'Luckily, I'm at the driver's side of the Ford, Harpur.'

'Luckily in which sense, sir?'

'In the sense that I can reach him quite easily. True, there are some glass shards and splinters sticking up in the bottom part of the window space but I don't want you to worry about me, Col, I'll go very gingerly when reaching in. Be sure I won't slash my wrists. You have that big, caring disposition and I would hate to give you unnecessary fret.'

'Thank you, sir.'

'I suppose you'll say that I shouldn't be reaching in at all, whether or not I can avoid the shards and splinters, because this will amount to interfering with evidence.'

'You shouldn't be reaching in at all, whether or not you can avoid the shards and splinters, because this will amount to interfering with evidence.'

'I prefer to see it as possibly *acquiring* evidence, Col. The garments of someone like Hart could be extremely fruitful.'

'In what sense, sir?'

'*You* wouldn't do it, would you, Col?'

'What?'

'Search him.'

'Obviously, he will have to be searched, sir, but probably these are not the correct circumstances. It requires Scenes of Crime people.'

'Fuck "correct circumstances", Harpur. I make my own circumstances. Who's going to correct me?'

'That's one of those questions we've spoken about before, isn't it, sir?'

'Which questions?'

'Rhetorical. They don't require an answer, because the answer is built in, usually negative. I think of Cain and Abel.'

'*What* do you think?'

'"Am I my brother's keeper?" Cain says when he's asked by God what's happened to Abel. Answer: "No", but unspoken, unnecessary.'

'I love the privacy of this kind of conversation, Col,' Iles replied.

'Which kind, sir?'

'Across the width of the Focus, you in your small aperture, I in mine. You're like a close-up on TV. This doesn't mean it offers any improvement on your appearance – the general shiftiness and signs of depravity are still evident – but it would need magic and a metric tonne of make-up to bring about even the most fragmentary change there, and the world in its kindly, tolerant way has grown used to you as you are. I agree.'

'Thank you, sir.'

'Our words remain enclosed, *in camera,* as it were, just you, me and a body. Of course, there are people about, some of them ours, some householders. But we are cordoned off, isolated, protected. Did you ever see *Fargo,* Col?'

'I'd bet that's a film, sir. There are a hell of a lot of films come out these days.'

'A snowy, cold setting. Two men standing very near each other in anoraks with their hoods up talk about the weather and it's almost as if the hoods are joined, so that they are holding the conversation from opposite ends of a short tunnel. That's how I see our well-ordered chat from frontal right to frontal left in this car, though, of course, we do have an additional item, Hart.' He shook his head, angrily but with restraint because of the shards and splinters. He'd be thinking of his jugular. 'Additional item. That's a disrespectful, patronizing phrase and I apologize, Col.'

'I'll gladly accept that on his behalf, sir. I'm sure he'd wish me to.'

'It's all the more disrespectful and patronizing because he is in some ways the truly important "item" of the three of us, isn't he, Harpur?'

'In what sense, sir?'

'He can tell us why he is here, in the close.'

'Well—'

'Oh, but you'll say he can't tell us this or anything else because he's dead as a result of coming into the close. That much we do know.'

'He can't tell us this or anything else because he's dead as a result of coming into the close. That much we do know.'

'Sharp of you, Col.'

'Thank you, sir.'

'When I speak of reaching in, what am I getting at, Col?'

'This is quite a question, sir, not rhetorical, but you'll know the answer to it.'

'Pockets, Harpur.'

'Ah.'

'Why I mentioned "fruitful". Perhaps, though, I should have said, "potentially fruitful". I like exactness, Col. I appreciate nuances.'

'You're famed for it, sir. Many's the time I've heard folk who've just talked with you say, "That Mr Iles, was there ever such a one for exactness and nuances?" (Answer, "No" – rhetorical).'

'Do you see what I'm getting at, Harpur?'

'In which respect?'

'"Potentially". Why I amended to that.'

'There'll definitely be a reason.'

'I referred to the fruitfulness of his garments, meaning pockets. But, obviously, Col, we cannot know what will be in those pockets until we've got our hands into them and discovered their contents.'

'Undeniable,' Harpur replied.

'And if we do not – cannot – know what is in them it is presumptuous to say the pockets will be "fruitful" in the sense I intended originally. Therefore a caveat type word is required – "potentially". His pockets might or might not provide us with helpful information. An imponderable at present.'

'I think I understand.'

'Some people, coming on an exploit of this kind, the Cairn Close kind, would empty their pockets before starting so that, should things go wrong – as in this case one might admit they rather *have* gone wrong – there will be nothing that gives a clue as to the details and purpose of the operation. Although Hart seems to have ignored some of the elementary precautions when entering the close, this does not mean he has ignored *all* precautions. And so we need "potentially", Col, and why I feel entitled to do a little tour of his pockets now as a priority, skirting all those well-intentioned but footling rules about what is and isn't permissible at the scene of a crime. I amuse myself now and then by thinking that the initials of my rank, Assistant Chief Constable – ACC – could also stand for "Attention: Cut the Crap".'

'There's no reason why an assistant chief shouldn't play with his initials in private, I'd say.'

'Thank you, Col. I'd like you to notice alignment.'

'Which?'

'Hart's. He's bent forward but also a little in the direction of this side. He might have been trying to get to somewhere less exposed when the shooting started. The result is that when I open this door so as to get at his pockets, he might fall out on to the road. I will be unable to stop that because I'll have to be on the other side of the door, if you can visualize this situation, Harpur. For the body to tumble higgledy-piggledy in such fashion would be deeply undignified and even grotesque, also conspicuous. He could come to rest across my feet, which is a sensation I can do without, thank you, Harpur.

'And suppose I've, in fact, partly opened the door and sense that he's about to slide out. I might feel compelled to prevent this by attempting to re-close the door. I would most likely jam him between the door and its frame. No matter how well-meaning this reaction might be, Col, it would have considerable ghastliness about it – clamping him in this manner, particularly if it were his head and face pincered. And then what would be the next move? If I opened the door to relieve the pressure he would probably continue his fall towards the road, out of focus, some might say. But if I didn't do that I'd be stuck in a rather unpleasant tableau keeping the squeeze on a deado, unable to return to normal because you, in your miserably, timorous pedantic style would refuse to help by coming around to this side of the Focus and humping Hart back in.

'So what I'm going to do is lean in now without opening *my* door and shove the sod hard towards *yours*. You will keep that closed, please. It will support him, keep him in the sitting position. Then I'll get *my* door properly opened and can climb in alongside Hart and do a quick frisk. Do you know that scene in *The Godfather* where the corrupt cop has to search Michael Corleone for a weapon as they drive to a restaurant? It will be something akin to that, though the car won't be moving, of course, and Hart is dead. We'll beat *rigor* OK or some of his pockets will be hard to get at.'

Iles disappeared. There was suddenly no face at the broken window. When he rose back into view Harpur saw the ACC must have bent down to take a shoe off. He had a left foot, black, lace-up in his right hand now, probably his customary Charles Laity at about £350 a pair. Using seven or eight short-arm jabs with the heel he knocked out all the glass spikes in the low part of the window frame, then dropped the shoe into the Focus cabin. He leaned through the window gap and grasped Hart's jacket on each shoulder, pulled him back from the wheel, lifted him a couple of inches and pushed him across the car into the passenger seat and against that door. Iles was slight in build but very forceful when using his arms, or in head-butting.

Because of the violence, Hart's face swung around as if seeking Harpur's in the destroyed window and wanting to give and get a farewell kiss. Harpur felt proud that he had not instinctively pulled back from this faux affectionate approach by Hart. It would have been squeamish, disrespectful, even cruel. Hart had a square, strong-jawed, normally lively face, but it had been part dismantled by at least one bullet which had taken away part of his right nostril and right cheekbone. His left shoulder rested on the passenger door now after Iles's powerful guidance and, as the ACC had forecast, he stayed sitting, did not slip to the floor. His eyes were dark blue and open.

Iles climbed in and sat behind the wheel. He bent forward and recovered his Charles Laity, put it on and re-tied the lace. Harpur thought the ACC might be sitting in blood and more of it would probably stain his uniform when he began the search of Hart's pockets. But Harpur knew that, having prioritized his trawl, Iles would accept the rough conditions. He'd said he created his own circumstances, and if one of the circumstances involved getting mucked up in blood, he'd get mucked up in blood.

Iles believed fiercely in logic when it chimed with what he wanted. He'd told Harpur a while ago that his favourite letters in the alphabet were Q E D. Naturally, Iles had assumed that Harpur didn't know what this combination meant, though Harpur, in fact, did. 'They're Latin, Col, *quod erat demonstrandum,* and are used when a mathematical problem has been satisfactorily solved, signifying, "Which was to be proved".' Tonight in Cairn Close what was to be proved was whether Hart had some give-away information in his pockets. Iles wouldn't let a bit of blood prevent this.

Hart had on a very superior looking brown jacket in soft leather and khaki chino trousers. Access to the jacket pocket nearest to Iles was simple and to the top and inside pockets. But for the coat pocket on the far side, Iles had to nestle in hard against Hart to cut distance. Half of the ACC's right upper body overlapped half of Hart's right upper body. This pressure on Hart caused a brief, rasping outgoing of air from his mouth. 'Speak up, old son,' Iles replied. To delve into the right and rear pockets of the trousers, Iles had to draw back a little, then resume his position part covering Hart for the left chino pocket. As he worked, Iles hummed what Harpur recognized as a rousing hymn, 'Hills of the North, Rejoice!'

Hart was obviously one of those people mentioned by the ACC who emptied their pockets at home before a possibly difficult operation. Iles found nothing. QED did apply, but un-favourably: it had been proved that Hart's clothes were not, in fact, 'fruitful'.

Iles disconnected himself from Hart and got out of the car. Then, with the door still open, leant in again, gripped the shoulders of the leather jacket once more and yanked the body back into the driver's seat. With gentle care Iles arranged him in a very authentic looking slouch over the wheel, his eyes towards Harpur across the car and seeming to ask, 'Pray who is this person settling me down with such gentle care?'

'Assistant Chief Iles,' Harpur answered.

'What, Col? Why suddenly so formal, you spectating poltroon?'

ELEVEN

Among members of my trade, and probably of some others – say, policing, fire fighting, bum-bailiffing – a very basic piece of folk wisdom preached caution: 'cherish your exit'. It meant, make sure before you move into what might become a dicey situation, that you know a way out; make sure, too, that this exit is not obstructed. To me, it always sounded defeatist: you'd be thinking of retreat even though you hadn't advanced one step.

And so the disaster at Cairn Close. I had it coming, and it came. Not a bad gravestone inscription that.

I don't want to turn heavy and psychological, but there has to be some attempt to explain how I decided it would be OK to drive into a dead-end. Yes, a very dead-end. It will be worth describing at some length, I'm afraid. Here goes, then: my trouble was that things up until Cairn had worked much too sweetly and easily for me. Ever since that tailing episode in the supermarket I'd grown to put absolute trust in my instincts. At that time, I'd had no training, no experience, of counter-surveillance and yet I'd spotted a way to lose Rory Mitchell who, I found out later, had been at that kind of activity for years; plus owning a first in anthropology from Cambridge.

As to education, my parents had gone more or less berserk when I told them I intended to quit school and take Bainbridge Williamson's offer of a job with Righton Private Inquiries. They had expected me to do what they had done, and what my brother and sisters had done – go to university, Oxbridge if possible, but somewhere else if not – and then start on a safe and progressive career. Part of my difficulty with them was that they didn't understand how I could have come to know the head of a private investigation firm. I'd thought it best not to tell them about Judith. She seemed to have lost interest in me when I left school, anyway. I think she'd got a special kick out of the maverick mischievousness of an affair with a pupil and didn't want to continue once

I'd turned adult enough to join the work force. A pity. She'd married not long after all that business with me and herself left the school to go and teach with her new husband in Wales somewhere.

For what he termed 'professional confidentiality considerations' Bainbridge wouldn't disclose to me who'd hired his firm to do the checks on Judith and me, but said he'd informed whoever it was that the agency had nothing conclusive to report about us, which in some ways was true: Rory had never been able to sneak up with a camera while we were in the back of the Honda.

A lot of my early work for Righton was fairly banal: missing person inquiries, divorce evidence, industrial espionage and/or vandalism, but the pay was fine and I reckoned to be earning more than my father after a year or so. This is what I'm getting at when I say I'd developed a trust in my own judgement and impulses. They seemed to get things right. Then came the partnership and even better money via a share of the profits. Rory resented being passed over and resigned. I did feel a quota of sympathy for him, but, of course, I also felt some triumph in seeing off the opposition.

The firm began to take on bigger and more complicated assignments. I thought I deserved some of the credit for that. I believed I could handle almost any commission, with or without Bainbridge. This might sound vain and if so, I'm sorry, but he and the private dick course had taught me brilliantly well how to analyze a situation on my own and deal with it on my own. I called it confidence, rather than vanity, but, then, I would, wouldn't I – to adapt a famous phrase from a London sex and politics trial years ago?

Above all I liked fine arts cases. There were plenty of these. It was estimated that about £300 million paintings and sculptures were thieved in a year in the UK alone. Expert firms ran elaborate databases that tried to keep track of great works, and offered their services to auction houses and insurance companies. We could be involved in several ways. For instance, collectors sometimes needed discreet, urgent help in tracing and getting back intact works stolen from them, though, for private reasons, they didn't want the police involved. Very private reasons. We never pressed to know them. Bainbridge said they were not relevant.

Our task was to search and find. If the client told us how the work had been acquired and it sounded credible we'd accept his/ her version unless and until something showed it to be bullshit. And if the client didn't tell us how the work had been acquired we assumed crookedness at some point or points in the purchase and/or in the run-up to the purchase.

Galleries and museums might ask for similarly discreet investigation of the provenance – the history – of a work or works they were thinking of bidding for. We could manage that. The constant brisk climb in picture valuations caused extremely learned and extremely snotty disagreements between experts about the authenticity, or not, of some works, especially the 'or not' sort. Between the allegedly fake and the allegedly jonnock piece there could be a cost gap of millions sterling: grounds for merciless ding-dong dog-fighting. In this kind of dispute, we might be hired to help one side or the other with deep, not always scrupulous, digging. There'd been quite an amount of dubious developments in the city lately centred on a prominent dealer in pictures, Jack Lamb.[2] And some aspects of that brought us interesting and very profitable work.

Money-lust and genuine artistic appreciation overlapped in this career, and the absence of clean-cut dividing lines tickled me. Some pictures might be famed for their vivid colouring, but, at the same time, might inhabit that foggy, grey area between lasting loveliness and an extremely meaty cash asking price. Weird. Great for a thinking-guy's mental playground.

This intriguing double nature of the firm's activities was what drew me, so up-beat and determined and big-hearted, to Cairn Close that evening. Maybe 'cockalorum' is another word that should feature somehow on my headstone: pride close to stupid, self-destructive arrogance.

2 See *Blaze Away*

TWELVE

Iles said, 'Contradictions, Col.'

'What type, sir?'

'Psychological.'

'A wide area.'

'To do with humans only.'

'Well, yes, I think I'd have expected that, given the circumstances.'

'Which circumstances?'

'These,' Harpur replied.

'Col, we have someone careful enough, savvy enough, professional enough, to clear his person of everything that might give away his purpose in coming here, but who then drives himself to a spot where he is exposed to an enfilade attack on both flanks via Focus side windows with no hope of striking back or, in fact, of surviving; he carried no armament. How do we reconcile these conflicting attitudes: the cagey, the crazy? It's what I mean by "contradictions". This is a psychology at, as it were, war with itself, one decision countering another.'

'My mother used to sing a number called "Undecided Now".'

'I didn't know you had a singing mother.'

'Singing at home, privately, while, say, cooking a fry-up. Not a diva in a hall.'

'Mothers unquestionably have their own roles to play in a household, Col.'

'Few would deny this.'

'Which idiotic, sectionable few?'

'My mother went on to more rousing songs: "Drake he's in his hammock",' Harpur replied. 'That kind of thing. "John Brown's Body". If you're interested I could put a list of her titles on paper for you.'

'I see hubris, Col.'

'Where, sir?'

'Hubris prompted him to come here.'

'Hubris was wrong to do that. It's irresponsible.'

'Hubris is not a person. I'm sorry, Col; clearly, I shouldn't
have expected you to know this word. Let's phrase it differently,
shall we?'

'Thank you, sir.'

'I see a kind of foolish, headstrong arrogance. It's as though
he said to himself, "OK, I'll do the routine preparatory bit –
vacuum cleaning my pockets – because this shows I'm aware of
hazard, am not naïve and/or blind. But I don't allow this awareness to scare me so much that I fail to act.'

They talked near the Focus and watched detectives knocking
doors in a search for witnesses. 'Of course, you, exercising your,
in some ways, admirable feet-on-the-ground style, Harpur, will
reply that if he'd prepared himself for something by pocket clearance – namely, the Cairn Close visit – it's surely not a contradiction to go and carry out the something which he'd prepared
himself for. In fact, it was rather the logical *result* of the preparation, or we have to ask why was he carrying out the preparation
for this something at all?'

'If he'd prepared himself for something by pocket clearance
– namely, the Cairn Close visit – it's surely not a contradiction
to go and carry out the something which he'd prepared himself
for. In fact, it was rather the logical result of the preparation, or
we have to ask why was he carrying out the preparation for this
something at all?'

'Shrewd, Col. Subtle. I couldn't have put this matter better
myself. But it isn't the whole picture, is it?'

'Isn't it?'

'At my rank, Harpur, I have to take a more general, a more
over-arching view. Because he saw the need for those crisis
preparations we can deduce he sensed something might turn
extremely rough and deleterious in his visit to the close, otherwise
there would be no reason for him to foresee a situation where
someone searches his clothes: this implies death or at least uncon-
sciousness. Why didn't he decide, therefore, that the whole project
was too risky? It would have been entirely possible for him,
entirely reasonable, to get hit by second thoughts and systematically, accurately, replace in their various correct pockets the items
he had previously removed as preparation. These might have

included material – notes, for instance – which referred to Cairn
Close and disclosed his reason for going there.

'Plainly, he didn't do that. If he'd grown scared as he contem-
plated the dangers, and abandoned any intention to come to the
close, there would be no occasion for me to meet him tonight,
alive or dead, let alone go through his pockets and feel around
his body for a holstered pistol. Neither he, nor I, nor you, Col,
would have been at Cairn Close now. And if, as it appears, out
of a kind of daft dauntlessness and pride, he opted to visit the
close, regardless of the recognized perils, he would empty his
pockets and keep them empty, particularly making sure he left
nothing in them that indicated why he had come to the close,
such as, say, notes as previously mentioned.

'So, whatever his response to the Cairn Close project, there
will be an unbridgeable gap in our information which we must
acknowledge and accept. We can only guess that he was driven
by some inane belief that bad fortune couldn't touch him. Where
would that fatal thought come from? Why?'

'This is where the hubris kicks in, is it, sir?' Harpur replied.
'As we know, he'd risen fast in his career. Perhaps it made him
over-bold, reckless, foolhardy. Hubris had been lurking around,
waiting for a likely customer and now Thomas Wells Hart arrives.'

'Brinkmanship, Col.'

'Brinkmanstiff.'

An elderly couple had emerged from one of the houses, number
8, and stood in their driveway observing the police at work.
Officers hadn't reached number 8 yet. Iles stepped towards them
and very amiably showed his blood-covered hands and wrists. 'I
wonder if I might come in and do a bit of sprucing of these in
your cloakroom?' he said. 'I'm sure such fine dwellings must
possess cloakrooms. As you'll probably realize we have something of a blip to deal with tonight and I felt it right to do a
standard rummage around in the Ford. Thus the inconvenient
consequence, however.' He nodded down at the blood.
'Additionally, I feel a dampness on my left buttock, which I don't
believe to be self-produced; also, as you can see, there's a
Tasmania-shaped stain on the left chest region of my uniform.
But I don't need to bother you about those extra problems. They
are by-the-way only.

'I dislike walking around with my hands in such a gaudy state, though. A little water clears me of this bleed, as Lady Macbeth almost said. Should a towel be involved, Harpur here will see it is properly laundered and returned to you, plus a note of thanks from the chief constable, within twenty-four hours. Harpur is great at ablutions-related problems. Washing-day skills are referred to resoundingly on his personnel records at headquarters. If he ever got to Staff College, which, naturally, he won't, his nickname would be "Mr Clean". Nicknames are very much a feature of Staff College. They will amusingly encapsulate people's major characteristics, acute, yet playful, and, admittedly, sometimes hostile; an unpleasant chaplain to the college when I was there had the cognomen "Mission Creep".'

'This occurrence is extremely unusual for the close,' the man said. He was in a green and white kimono type robe with a chunky necklace of wooden beige and brown beads, suede desert boots, and a red woollen bobble hat on a very good head of grey hair, nicely brushed back over his ears. He was mid-height, burly, long-faced, his cheeks very thick and heavy looking. Harpur wondered if their weight would cause him to bend forward in a stoop as bodily strength lessened with further ageing. Apparently to show big disapproval he double-twitched the kimono on his shoulders and said, 'One doesn't expect this category of incident in such a normally tranquil setting.'

'You know, I can certainly believe that,' Iles replied. 'Probably rare, perhaps unique. If Ford Focuses regularly drove into the close and got a great blast of murderous gunfire aimed at them, we'd all have heard about it, not just people in the close, but throughout the city, even nationally, perhaps through mentions in the media. Property values could be affected. People would ask estate agents trying to flog one of the houses, "But isn't that the venue where Ford Focuses get repeatedly, ferociously fucked-up? Would our children be safe playing on the pavement? Isn't there bound to be unseemly noise?".'

'The gunfire you refer to is what I have in mind,' the man said.

'It's because of the gunfire that my hands are stained,' Iles replied in a mild, QED tone, showing them again. 'My hands would be in their normal condition if there had been no gunfire.

There is a definite causal link between the shooting and the present state of my hands. And although now there's a very, very breathless hush in the close tonight over at the Focus, we know it wasn't like that only a short time ago.'

'There might be some parts of the city where gunfire is customary – gangdom, pimp disputes, people caught in flagrante, turf battles etcetera – but not so Cairn Close,' the man said. 'It's hard to think of a reason for shooting in the close. "Who, but who, Felix, would wish to bring fusillades to Cairn?" Veronica asked me during the onslaught. I could give no satisfactory answer. No answer at all. Ironic that the vehicle should be a Focus. We focus on it yet learn nothing of its backstory.'

'If somebody had told me shots would be heard in the city tonight, I wouldn't have assumed Cairn Close was the most probable location,' Iles said. 'I don't know whether Harpur might think differently. He strikes out alone sometimes. You'll most likely find this hard to credit, but, yes, he can and does. I feel he's entitled to his own view of things, however obtuse, and it's good for his morale if he can think for a while that people respect his opinions.'

'We seek to preserve calm and to practise good neighbourliness in the close, though this doesn't mean nosying into one another's confidentialities,' Felix said.

'The point about this blood on my hands is that it's liable to get spread. Suppose, for instance, I push a lock of hair back from my forehead in an instinctive, automatic gesture,' Iles replied. He lifted his right hand to make a slightly mannered, though graceful, move illustrating the possible sequence, but did not actually touch himself. 'This might leave a disturbing crimson smudge on my brow.'

Felix said, 'Of the two of us, it was my wife who first noticed the violence in the close and spoke of it to me. I immediately dialled 999.' She was taller than her husband, hair cut very short and dyed auburn, strong straight nose, inquisitive brown eyes under thin brows, black leather bomber jacket, knee-length, roomy, orange shorts; Harpur thought they'd both be in their eighties.

He said, 'We have three names of emergency callers from Cairn: Aspen, Nape, Imperio.'

'Nape,' Nape said.

'Could you describe what you saw when the shooting began outside, Mrs Nape?' Harpur said. 'Did you notice people leaving the second car, possibly at a rush, and possibly holding handguns? We are assuming, I think, that there were at least two people carrying out the attack, one for each side of the Focus. They might have had balaclavas on, though, of course, that would signal to anyone who spotted them before the actual shooting that they had some illegality in mind.'

'Are you going to let me wash off this sodding stuff?' Iles said.

'That's all very well, but we don't want to get drawn into anything,' Felix said. 'I think I speak for Veronica as well as myself. It would look as if we were taking sides, providing facilities.'

'I don't ask that the water should be warm,' Iles replied.

'We would object, Veronica and I, to find our home described in the press as a kind of staging post offering relief to one of the factions. And then a possible letter from the chief constable. Word of this might get out, branding us collaborators.'

'I'll draft a letter for him to send you, Felix,' Iles replied. 'It will say you're the arsehole of all arseholes, congratulate you on the supreme arseholeness of your arseholeness. You can show it to reporters as happy proof that you are not on our side, or we are not on yours, anyway.'

THIRTEEN

I would have liked the chance to tell Judy Vasonne that she mustn't blame herself for those moments of acute devilishness in Cairn Close. But no, things happened too fast and too terminally. The acute devilishness was *so* acute that it offered me no opening to send a comforting dispatch. She would certainly have heard about the ambush and might feel responsible. After all, wasn't it because of her that I'd taken this PI job and its risks; risks most probably absent from a career in feet? I would almost certainly never have encountered Bainbridge Williamson and the Righton agency if Rory hadn't tried to tail me on my way home after being with Judith. She was a kind of midwife in all this, but one bringing death not new life.

Judith had led me towards that close catastrophe in another much more obvious and direct way, too. I don't mean she did this deliberately. Of course she didn't. Although she liked japes and merry ruses, that would be beyond. She did help create the Cairn situation, however, no question. And she was sure to know she did. She'd have big regrets and reproach herself mercilessly. Judith could be like that. There was the wild side, as with the zoom-zoom chiropody papers, and the special sex requirements – 'Pray shag the arse off me, you school kid'– but she also slid into gloom now and then, her sparky, aggressive confidence temporarily gone. That seemed natural to me for someone who had to live with all the Old Testament grief, pain and blame as a religious education teacher. Think of Job and the plague of boils; or King Belshazzar, Neb's son, told by a mysterious finger writing on the walls of the banqueting hall in the middle of a knees-up that he had been weighed in the balances and found wanting, but not through anorexia.

It was a surprise to hear from Judy again. How long would it be since I'd seen her? Six, getting on for seven, years? Now, she called on my office phone and said, 'Tom, how are you, my dear?' This I didn't much go for. I reckoned the 'my dear' had been carefully picked and deployed to set an altered tone between her and me: not a soulmate's hot phrase but an old-pal-to-old-pal's greeting, anti-hormonal. In fact, she spoke it as 'm'dear' rather than 'my dear', as if to downplay any idea of loving possession, her of me, I of her. She said, 'I'm glad you're still with the firm that changed everything back then. I resented it at the time – took you away, didn't it, kiboshed unilaterally one of my sweet naughtinesses? I'm all right with it now. And, what's more, I might have some business for you.'

The call reached me via the Righton switchboard and if the operator listened in I wondered what she'd make of 'kiboshed unilaterally one of my sweet naughtinesses'. I had a secure, direct, private line, of course, It came with the directorship, years after I had lost contact with Judith and she couldn't know the number. She did know the name of the company I'd quit school to join and must have found Righton in a directory or ad describing our services. I said, 'Judith! Lovely to hear your voice. Where are you?'

'Not far off. Did I ever mention my brother?'

'Big modern house out towards Rastelle Major on the edge of the city? A sister-in-law, nephews and nieces?'

'I visit now and then.'

'Oh! You've been often hereabouts but never got in touch until today? Why so?'

'At times I wanted to. But it didn't seem right.'

'Not right how?'

'Like trying to bring the past back. Unwise. Sad. Tempting. But too much has intervened. I'm extremely married. And what about you, Tom? Married, too? Or, at least, I expect there's someone el . . . Or at least I expect there's someone.'

She'd obviously been going to say 'someone else', but had stopped herself. The 'else' would mean that although she, Judith, was still the major woman in my life there was, also, this 'someone else'.

'No, not married,' I said. 'But, yes, there's someone.'

'Of course. Natural.'

I saw she meant to keep the conversation terse, unemotional, detached, breezy. She wouldn't ask the someone's name, let alone details about her personality, age and/or appearance. I had the idea she was ferociously interested in all of that and therefore made sure she didn't show it.

'Things are different, aren't they, Tom?' she said. 'As I explained, this is a business call. It's about him – Keith, my brother.'

'He's doing all right, isn't he? Wasn't his business design, décor, that kind of thing?'

'I think he's moving into some dark realms. Or has moved there already.'

'Which dark realms?'

'This could leave him and his family very exposed and vulnerable. Very unsafe. We're talking about three children as well as him and his wife.'

'"Exposed and vulnerable" how?'

'Can we meet? This needs some face-to-face,' she replied.

'Delighted. How about The Knoll eatery opposite the station? I'll buy you lunch.'

'No need for that.'

'If it's business it'll be on expenses. Proves I'm working. Entertaining prospective client.'

'Oh, right. Proves who to?'

'Me. I'm a partner-director here now.'

'Yes. Congrats.' Thirty seconds' silence. Then she seemed to reach the guts of what she wanted to say. 'You'll be used to some . . . well, some danger, I imagine.'

Her tone said she hoped so, and that this was the only reason she'd phoned me. 'Limited,' I said. 'I'm not Chandler's Philip Marlowe.'

What the fuck had Keith been up to, might still be up to? The little pause before 'well, some danger,' signalled, didn't it, that if I agreed to take on this job I would probably again run into 'some danger'.

She fixed the meeting for next day. We could never have gone like this, openly, to a local restaurant in our previous time together. That wouldn't have qualified as Judith's 'sensibly discreet'. To be seen walking the street together needn't have been a give-away: it could be that pupil and teacher bumped into each other and out of normal social ease had strolled a little distance in company. But a meal in a restaurant, with cosy menu discussions, forked morsel swapping and wine, maybe, was sure to have signalled something deeper. In any case, I couldn't have afforded restaurant treats then and would have felt damn lowly and pitiable if I'd let her pay. I was a schoolboy, but a schoolboy who preferred not to be reminded of it when doing lunch with a lover.

Now I could stand her the meal, or Righton could, and not worry on her behalf at being noticed. Oddly, though, I found I didn't altogether care for this. I'd enjoyed the thrill that came with secrecy with furtiveness, even if these had kept us out of The Knoll. Immature, really. Just the same, I think I half wished it could still be like that. It couldn't. As she'd said, 'Unwise.' Nostalgia stayed nostalgia. Six years plus brought changes. Six years plus crushed juvenile romantic excitement. Yes, I regretted it. Business lunches at The Knoll were routine, were workaday.

Not that she *looked* workaday now, unless being splendidly elegant, splendidly beautiful, was work. Other customers glanced up when she walked into The Knoll, then glanced down to their plates in case their gazing seemed rude, then glanced back again, having obviously decided that what was on the plates, no matter how tastefully arranged, couldn't come close to matching Judith for loveliness. And they turned this second glance into a stare, rude or not.

As host, I was already at a table. I got to my feet, honoured to claim her and monopolize her, even if it *were* only business. She had on a navy textured blazer with revere collar and horn-effect buttons. She wore this over a white, cotton, round-necked tunic. Her thigh-hug trousers had a jacquarded dense floral pattern worked into the dark-blue background weave. She carried a sizeable brown leather handbag. Fashion, I knew a fair whack about by now. As part of the private investigator course Bainbridge sent me on soon after I joined the firm, there'd been a module devoted to clothing and its descriptive terms, men's and women's, for use in tracing and missing person cases. Bainbridge would be easy to trace if he stuck with those long, flapping jackets.

Not many of the tracing and missing person cases involved people with features like Judith's though, nor with jacquarded trousers cosseting longish, flawless legs. I gave her a kiss on the cheek. Well, she'd spoken of a 'face-to-face' occasion. This should sodding-well suit, shouldn't it? *Shouldn't it???* That formal, sexlesss peck defined how things were now.

I realized that behind the vapid politesse and whiff of Allure – from her – each of us would be scrutinizing the other for signs of change; hoping with disgustingly egomaniac cruelty to seem better preserved. Most probably I was the one who'd altered most. Last time we met I'd been a youth. Now, I was a man, wearing one of a dozen made-to-measure shirts from my wardrobe, and in a career impressive enough for her to come asking for support. Some family crisis had forced her to end the stand-off between her and me and decide that 'm'dear' Tom might be able to sort it. Well, 'm'dear Tom' had dealt with other crises, some family, some not, so I might know how to oblige effectively now. I'd put on about ten or twelve pounds since we last met, but that was OK. I'd needed a little extra weight. I stood 5' 11" and it was evenly spread.

And Judith? She must be twenty-seven or eight now, her skin as fresh and lineless as before, her brunette hair thick and glossy, down in plentiful mass to her shoulders, her eyes brown, full of curiosity and challenge, her nose neat, snubwards but not altogether. She'd moved with easy, big strides across the restaurant to join me. She was around 5' 7" on moderate heels, slim, her breasts as I remembered them, and certain today, as much as in the past, to buck me up. The meal with her and perhaps some wine would also do this, but they were accessories only.

She wore an unnaturally broad wedding ring, very binding; one of those things that had 'intervened'. A slap across the chops with her shapely left hand might knock an enemy's front teeth out. Her own front teeth were pleasantly uneven and very strong looking. Clearly they could give a formidable bite, but she'd always been very careful and skilled with her mouth where it might have caused wounds and permanent untidy scarring.

I always used to think Judith's behind too gorgeous to be merely sat on, yet she did, of course, sit on it, and she gracefully sat on it now in The Knoll. I would bet I wasn't the only one there who tried to visualize the thigh, hip and loins details of that movement and the eventual caressing, undercarriage contact with the chair.

'Do I seem like something of a nanny, Tom?'

'I don't think I've ever seen anyone who looked less like a nanny,' I said.

'I mean, fretting about my brother, poking into his life on the quiet, as if he can't look after himself.'

'You think he can't?'

'I don't know. It's one of the reasons I've come to you.'

'You don't want me simply to find out what he's doing, but to get an idea of whether he can cope with what he's doing?' I said.

'His judgement might have gone askew. He's got the big house and, I imagine, a big mortgage. He's got a wife who likes to spend. He's got three children at private schools. There might be a need for quick money. Possibly he thinks he's found one.'

'Legal?'

'Maybe.'

'But maybe not?'

'Possibly.'

'In design?'

'Related.'

She ordered half a dozen oysters and then veal. I chose sardines followed by steak and kidney pie. We had a half bottle of Chablis and a half of red Burgundy.

She said, 'My parents are so proud of him, Tom. They'd be poleaxed if he came unstuck. He's their eldest child. They regard him as a figurehead. They're obsessed about family reputation. I'm not sure what they make of me, or what they'd have made of me if they knew everything. Perhaps my fussing over Keith is a kind of sub-conscious recompense to them.'

'Steady, Judith. "Unstuck" how?'

'I don't know exactly. That's why I need you.'

'So, what *do* you know?'

'I pick up persistent hints from Olive, his wife. She's less guarded with me than he is. She seems to think any talk is inside the family so no need to be uptight.'

'Talk about what?'

'To do with art – pictures. Plus maybe sculptures.'

'To do with them how?'

She shook her head, a slight, puzzled sort of movement. 'Olive says there was big trouble lately at a rather dodgy dealer's place.'

'Jack Lamb's.'[3]

'That's the name. Attempted robbery and a death.'

'Yes.'

'So police swarming there at the time and on super-alert since for any aftermath. I gather that certain late-stage buying and selling was interrupted by all this activity and general chaos. Some valuable items that were in transit or were about to be in transit had to be put on hold. They might or might not have been of dubious history, disputable provenance. What Olive seemed to be saying was that Keith fancied he saw a chance for anyone smart and determined in this breakdown of normal commerce.'

'Keith?'

'That's the way she figures it.'

'A chance how?'

'I don't think she has any notion of that. She seemed to believe it would all be so simple for anyone smart and determined.'

'Keith.'

'Can you have a peek at it, Tom?'

Peek. That was supposed to make it sound routine, even trivial. Her voice shook slightly, though. Her face was for a few moments miserable, perhaps touched by fright. She didn't meet my eyes.

'We're not cheap,' I said.

'I've got savings. I'll pay.'

'But as you're a virtual creator of one half of the firm there might be a decent discount.'

'Thanks.'

'Talking of which, what happened to that evil piece who put us under surveillance – or whom you thought put us under surveillance?'

'I hear she left her husband and went off with a married sex therapist, kind of coals to Newcastle.'

3 See *Blaze Away*

FOURTEEN

Yes, with its wines and oysters and steak and kidney, and the opportunist Knoll chair snug beneath Judith's mesmerizing, unbulky arse, this stately luncheon would lead on and on and on and eventually to Cairn Close and dumdum closure. At the time, though, it was the arrant vagueness of what she'd said and its lush melodrama that I noticed most. Well, I ask you, who wouldn't? 'Some danger', 'dark realms'. Dark *fucking* realms? She couldn't define them, gazetteer them, couldn't specify the danger, or describe clearly and credibly how her brother hoped to cash in on that terrible mess-up at Jack Lamb's place – the 'art' element in her worries. She relied on 'hints' from her sister-in-law. 'Hints' meant guesses.

Another module on the PI course had dealt ferociously with the difference between evidence and fantasy and the need for all operatives to recognize when a moment of speculation and imagination might be useful, but also – this more crucial – to spot when it became stupidly distracting. The lecturer had said, 'Of course, you'll all know the Keats' line, "Ever let the fancy roam." Yes, let it roam, over the cliff.' The sister-in-law, Olive, seemed to believe Keith would descend on the chaotic pics and sculptures trade after that Lamb upheaval and pick his way through it to ample and gorgeous gains. Oh, yea? What was that other figment from Keats – 'realms of gold'?

However, I felt I couldn't refuse Judith. I reckoned she had a reasonable claim on me, including the new me, because of those distant days. They still counted, despite the hawser-width wedding ring and all the other changes that had 'intervened' during the last six or seven years. Her breasts stayed brilliantly persuasive. I *would* take the 'peek' or two into the Keith problem, but perhaps not more than that. I'd try to discover fast that there was, in fact, nothing much to find out about him, except that he had what seemed to be a nicely profitable business, or nicely profitable businesses, somewhere, with nothing at all criminal about it or them: no dark, satanic realms. QED.

Out of kindness, I'd tried to keep any trace of amused disbelief out of my face as she spoke of her own and Olive's suspicions. Just the same, she seemed to sense that I regarded most of what she'd said so far as woolly and hysterical. I could tell she aimed to counter this. She would get precise and particular, she would get concrete. We were at the coffee stage of our meal and she brought from her handbag what looked like a large, folded sheet of drawing paper. She opened it to full size and spread it between us on the lunch table. I saw what appeared to be two pencilled blueprints of the interior of a building, showing rooms, corridors, doors, windows. She pointed to one of the drawings. 'Upstairs,' she said, then moved her finger to the other. 'Downstairs and garden-cum-grounds.'

'What is it?' I said, knowing what it was.

'Failsafe.'

'Being?'

'Its name: Olive and Keith's house.'

'Yes?'

'Actually, I don't think we need the upstairs. But I thought it best to be thorough. So I sketched both.'

She kept her voice down. I had understood why. She was talking to me about a possible break-in, wasn't she? That's how it looked; preposterous, of course, but, apparently, not to her.

'This room,' she said and put her finger on a small rectangle at the top left edge of the downstairs diagram. 'It's where he sees people, more or less remote from the busy parts of the house. There's a direct way into it from an outside concrete path and patio. They rarely use the main front door.'

'Which people?'

'Because of how things are arranged, I don't see many of them. But occasionally I've spotted one or two coming from or going back to their cars. They seem expensively dressed, the men as well as the women. The cars are mostly Range Rovers, but also a Merc and a Lexus sometimes. I don't think the door to the corridor is locked, but it seems recognized as private by Olive – and by the children if they are around. And by me, naturally. The door at the other end, opening on to the patio and garden certainly *is* locked except when one of Keith's meetings is taking place.'

'So what are the meetings about? What's going on?'

'Have you been taught how to bug a place?' she replied.

Yes, I'd been taught how to bug, though not a place, a car, and not on the PI course. Bugging a place could be illegal. No respectable training company would have it on their syllabus. I'd learned what I possessed of this skill from Bainbridge Williamson. Where *he'd* learned it I didn't know or need to. I'd had one failed attempt and, subsequently, two very successful buggings. But Righton used this ploy only sparingly. The risk of discovery was acute. And, in any case, what was discovered through a bugging had to be employed with great care and subtlety, to disguise how it had been got. Evidence obtained by bugging could not be used direct in court because it might have been acquired illegally. On account of these possible snags and hazards bugging of property was restricted to very major cases, and done by Bainbridge himself: generally divorces of the rich, or exposure of industrial espionage, when Williamson would occasionally decide the fees to Righton warranted the gamble.

Judith's project couldn't be treated as very major. She wanted to discover if her brother was deep into some kind of criminal trading. Suppose I proved that he was, she would presumably confront him, and try to make him stop. She didn't want their parents hurt and shamed, and they would be if Keith messed up somehow and his crookedness came to light. Admittedly, this showed a nice concern for the parents, but I couldn't give it very much weight.

Judith intended staying at her brother's place for a fortnight while her husband was abroad somewhere on an education freebie. I reckoned this would give me time to dig out enough on Keith to make her realize how crazed her suggestion about bugging Failsafe was, and how crazed her suspicions were about him altogether.

She pointed again at the downstairs plan. 'Here's the door on to the gravelled path and patio. I should be able to make sure it was unlocked when the room's not occupied. I expect you're used to working swiftly in selecting a site and fixing the device, Tom, aren't you?'

FIFTEEN

There were times when Harpur couldn't be certain whether Iles was skittishly sending himself up; or whether he had an inborn, irresistible, taste for the grandiose. Either way, it could result in a touch of the florid in his conversation. 'Conversation' would possibly be the wrong word if it meant an exchange of talk. 'Statement' might be better. Or even 'spiel'.

Now, for instance, he said, 'Madam, there will have been few, if any, occasions in the past when an assistant chief constable, brackets, Operations, has stood on this doorstep of an evening and rung your bell. In the crude but illuminating words of the present day demotic this is a "one-off". The reason and cause are in that seemingly tagged-on, subordinate term, "Operations". My area of responsibility within this city's police force is, as it happens, operations. Harpur here will bear me out. That is one of his limited flairs – bearing me out.'

'Assistant Chief Iles *is* Operations,' Harpur said.

'Thank you, Col,' Iles said. 'This lady might not be familiar with my ACC epaulettes insignia, though you and I know it to be meaningful and authentic. The blood on my hands and uniform will probably strike her as unusual and, possibly, disconcerting, but you and I both know, also, that there is a very simple explanation for it.'

'Very simple, sir. Thomas Wells Hart's heart.'

'True. Now, when a Ford Focus and its driver, Thomas Wells Hart, are shot-up in a normally quiet, sedate close, the police response will obviously amount to an operation. Therefore, that response will be led by an assistant chief constable, brackets, Operations, viz, myself. But you, madam, will probably reply that assistant chiefs don't normally take on such low-grade, street-level duties as house-to-house inquiries, even though the house-to-house inquiries are plainly part of a police operation and therefore fall within the ambit of an ACC, brackets, Operations. You might say that such an operation would probably be run from a Command Vehicle, constructed for that purpose, or from a Tactical Control Centre with many screens and sophisticated communication systems at headquarters itself.

'This is a perfectly sound argument, and I congratulate you on your clear-sightedness. However, my companion here, Harpur, will tell you that when an operation seems to have special, perhaps symbolic, global qualities, the ACC will wish to involve himself in the most basic, nitty-gritty aspects of the case. He needs and demands contact with its core, its central fibre. This assistant chief is an all-shoulders-to-the-wheel assistant chief, including his.'

Harpur said, 'When an operation seems to have special, perhaps symbolic, global qualities the ACC will wish to involve himself in the most basic, nitty-gritty aspects of the case. He needs and demands contact with its core, its central fibre. This assistant chief is an all-shoulders-to-the-wheel assistant chief, including his.'

'Again, very true, Col,' Iles replied. 'As an example, madam, of this tilt towards the nitty-gritty and central fibre we have just had a vastly dud chin-wag with that oozy, kaftan prat at number 8. And now, as you'll observe, we have moved on and favour the expectation that you will not turn out to be such an all-time jerk as ratbag Felix. A harmless request in the pursuit of hygiene was rejected. He chooses to pass bile on the other side.'

'We wondered whether you'd seen anything in the close around the time of the shooting, before, during or after, but especially before,' Harpur said. 'Preparations. Reconnaissance of the ground.'

'I live alone here,' she replied.

'And that's why I'm not going to ask if I could come in and wash my hands,' Iles said. 'You don't want a male stranger – in off the street, unannounced – splashing about in your cloakroom and possibly bringing residue stains to an innocent towel.'

'Please,' she said. 'We should, as it were, reach out generously to those finding themselves suddenly in our neighbourhood and requiring help. On the right. You'll find many different kinds of soap present, used by me for a freshening up or full-scale ablution. I will select a soap which, in my judgement, matches a mood of the moment via shape, texture and scent. A mojo matter.

If you are in difficulty deciding which of the ranged soaps harmonizes with *your* current feelings, pray give me a shout, and I'll come and describe for you the distinctive afflatus of each bar. My belief is that almost any type will get rid of the blood but I'm thinking of the wind-down aftermath of that cleansing session.'

The woman stood aside and Harpur and Iles entered the house. Iles made for the cloakroom. Harpur said, 'I've had a look at the Cairn Close electoral register on my mobile and it gives the occupant of this property as Millicent Helen Groves.'

'Mrs. Divorced.' She took Harpur into a lounge full of shining, metal-framed furniture, with vivid upholstery in prime colours. There were large, framed black and white urban scene photographs on the walls: a dog looking out of a window; a washing line with long socks and other clothes drying; what might be a Greek orthodox church interior; boys on the edge of a lake or pool launching a toy yacht. Mrs Groves and Harpur sat opposite each other. Harpur thought she'd be in her late fifties. She had on a navy business suit, a mauve blouse, black high heels. 'It's true, Felix can be a bit of a cunt,' she said. 'He's in therapy and has been for an age but there's an inherent, congenital, perhaps inherited, awfulness about him that no psychiatrist can properly fight without systematically destroying Felix as Felix. This might seem desirable, but Felix is rather too fond of being Felix, and keeps reverting to his natural odiousness. *Nostalgie de la boue* – "Let me get back to my slime."'

Iles rejoined them. Joyfully he declared, 'I seemed to bind more or less immediately with a pale yellow soap, fifth from the left, a swift, mutual empathy, so I had no need to summon help.' He held up his clean hands as in a surrender gesture. It would be a surrender to the elementary washing efficiency of the soap but also to its grander, spiritual, tonic power. 'Have my hands ever been more taint free? I can reply with a resounding "No", thanks to that particular ministering soap.' He toured the room slowly looking at the photographs. 'There's something about long socks on a line, isn't there?'

'In which respect, sir?' Harpur said.

'Oh, yes,' Iles replied with an unhurried, gentle, this-is-life-as-it's-lived chuckle.

'No, I saw nothing before the shooting,' Mrs Groves said. 'Harpur would mean not just pre the shooting this evening, but anything over the last few days that might have had you thinking a Ford Focus and its driver would be getting a fusillade here soon.'

'No, nothing like that,' she said.

'I name a Ford Focus because we now know that it *was* a Ford Focus blitzed here tonight,' Iles replied. 'But, clearly, your intimations at that pre-incident stage would not necessarily specify a Ford Focus because you wouldn't have the full, actual picture. Your intimations might figure some disaster involving almost any kind of car, a wholly random itemizing, say a Vauxhall or Skoda.'

'No, nothing of that sort,' she replied. 'I don't think I've ever seen a Skoda in this close.'

Iles said, 'The Skoda I cited was not intended to be a *factual* Skoda. Simply I meant some non-Ford Focus, such as, for instance, a Skoda. Any make would have done, other than a Ford Focus – Vauxhall, Peugeot, Lexus, Mercedes, VW, BMW, you choose.'

'Mr Iles is famed for employing his own way of coming at things,' Harpur said in the kind of friendly voice he often chose when decoding Iles's frenzied quirks for strangers. 'I've heard people who've just met and listened to him comment afterwards something like, "That Mr Iles, he's entitled to be how he is, but it must take a lot of work". He'd have that Skoda or Vauxhall very clearly in his mind, but this is the veritable nub, isn't it? They are *in his mind* only, whereas the Ford Focus will arrive as something very real and riddled.'

'Obviously, when I heard the shooting I took notice,' Mrs Groves said. 'I'd not long come in from work and was having tea in the kitchen. But because of the sudden racket I went to the front window, not knowing what I might see.'

'But not a Skoda,' Iles said.

'Three people, most likely two male, one female, running back from the dark saloon car towards the Ford Focus. Behind the Focus a black estate car had blocked off the mouth of the close.'

'Weapons?' Harpur asked.

'Too distant and dark to see,' she said.

'So you can't describe faces?' Harpur said.

'I was viewing them from behind,' she replied.

'Build?' Harpur said. 'Can you estimate age?'

'The front runner squat, wide-shouldered, thick-necked, probably thirties, early thirties, male. One of the pair following seemed younger, more athletic, tall – over six feet, but solid, not gangling, male. The other I thought, think, might have been a woman, mid-twenties, head well back, a jogging style, easy and relaxed, one foot hitting the ground in more or less the exact spot where the leading foot did. A *man's* feet won't usually form such a neat pattern when sprinting.'

'Someone running while holding a pistol, right or left according to preference, would probably have a different running style from someone *not* holding a pistol,' Iles said. 'It's unlikely to have looked "easy and relaxed". I believe the arm and hand with the gun would be kept stiff down at her/his side. Perhaps this one of the trio didn't do any of the shooting.'

'No heels, for the woman of course, if a woman,' Mrs Groves said. 'I think trainers.'

'This looks to me like a hastily planned, but very efficient operation,' Harpur said. 'She'd know – if it was a she – she'd know she will need to get clear fast, so she wears what's going to be convenient rather than fashionable, something that can help give the easy and relaxed style. After all, on the face of it, an easy and relaxed style would be tricky to manage after slaughtering Thomas Wells Hart. I suppose you wouldn't have been able to tell if they were masked.'

'No. She, if it was a she – had some kind of navy or black skull-cap on,' Mrs Groves said.

'So we've got no hair colour,' Harpur said.

'As you said, a skilled operation,' she replied.

'We meet skilled operations with Operations,' Iles replied. 'We meet skilled operations with the assistant chief constable (Operations). Me.'

Harpur said . . .

SIXTEEN

But why always Harpur?

SEVENTEEN

Well, let's get accurate: it *isn't* always Harpur. This time, though, it is. We'd better amend, 'But why always Harpur?' to 'Why *so often* Harpur?' Partly it's because he tries continually, valiantly, to make Iles comprehensible, tolerable and even likeable to those around and about; in fact, to make him comprehensible, tolerable and even likeable to the general populace. Harpur saw this as a kind of almost dazzlingly difficult grail mission, its importance hard to overstate. Hadn't he already attempted to humanize some of Iles for Mrs Millicent Helen Groves in her homely soap haven in the close; or, at least, humanize him as far as was feasible?

Now, Harpur had to take on a similar routine job with a much younger, grieving, desperate woman. 'Is it Tom?' she yelled. 'It's Tom, isn't it? But why? How can it be Tom?' Her voice filled the sealed-off suburban space. 'How? Oh, how, why?'

Iles said in that pleasantly ice-breaking tone he occasionally dug out from somewhere, 'You'll be Judith Vasonne, I expect.'

'How do you know that?' she replied.

'Or perhaps née Vasonne, but now something other,' Iles said.

'How do you know that?' she said.

'The ring's fairly gargantuan,' Iles said.

Harpur said, 'Mr Iles – that is, Assistant Chief Constable Iles – will sometimes have moments of revelation that come as an overwhelming surprise to those present, and possibly more than a surprise, a breathtaking shock.'

'Religious Education,' Iles said. 'And Careers.'

'What are they to do with it?' she said.

'With what?' Iles asked

'With this murder,' she said.

Harpur said, 'We have an incident here.'

'Of course you have a fucking incident. The incident is Tom shot to death, isn't it?' she said.

'Harpur likes to move slowly and with careful, calibrated vocab from established fact to subsequent established facts,' Iles said. 'It's laborious, yes, but perfectly valid for someone of his nature and abilities.'

He and Harpur had just left Mrs Groves. They were at the gate of her front garden and about to step on to the pavement. The close was taped-off at the entrance and guarded as a crime site, but the officer in charge there must have decided the woman had something useful to say and brought her to them.

'It was that miserable cow, was it?' she said.

'Which miserable cow?' Iles replied.

'In touch with you, then – spreading personal information.'

'Which person, or persons, plural?'

'Mine and Tom's. Most probably she'd do it unsigned. Sneaky. Evil. You got anonymous stuff through the post, did you?' she asked.

'Which anonymous stuff?' Iles replied.

'From the cow,' she said.

'Which cow?'

'The connection,' she said.

'What connection?' Iles said.

'You know what connection. How could you have my name like that if you didn't?'

'Mr Iles and connections – it's a similar story,' Harpur said. 'If a connection exists he'll spot it. He's like one of those sniffer dogs, though not with drugs but connections.'

'Whose blood is that on your gorgeous tunic, Iles?' she replied. 'Why was he here, in this damn shooting-gallery?'

'I think Harpur hoped *you'd* be able to tell *us* that,' Iles said.

'How would I be able to tell you?' she said.

'You got here very quickly,' Iles replied.

'Local radio said an attack. They mentioned a Ford Focus.'

'*You* made a connection?' Harpur said.

'You've seen him lately, have you?' Iles said. 'Things continue?'

'It *is* Tom, is it?' she asked.

'I can understand why you feel envious. Yes, I have his blood seeping through on to my chest. But I'm afraid, Judith, we can't let you get any nearer to the car,' Iles said. 'The whole close is non-access and non-exit except for our vehicles and the Focus is especially unapproachable. This is one of the basic police rules at a crime location.'

'You obviously approached it,' she said.

'But as Harpur will tell you, I'm me, and this makes an absolute difference.'

'Mr Iles is very much him,' Harpur said. 'He long ago saw off any competition. Our forensic people will be here soon and photographers, then a mortuary van.'

Harpur had driven himself and Iles to Cairn Close in an unmarked Range Rover. It was parked near the Ford Focus. The three of them – Judith Vasonne, Iles and Harpur – went to sit in it now and talk some more, Harpur at the wheel, Judith alongside him, Iles behind. 'You're living not far away, then?' Harpur said.

'I'm staying with my brother and sister-in-law near Rastelle Major, a break while my husband's abroad.'

'And have you been in touch with Thomas Wells Hart?' Iles said.

'We had lunch at The Knoll,' she said.

'For old times' sake?' Iles asked. 'How admirably commemorative!'

'Exactly,' she said.

'Nothing more?' Iles said.

'What more could there be?'

'There is clearly a strong, rather lovely bond between you even so long after that initial shag-happy time when he and you were still at school, so to speak. Your distress and all that bellowing of the "hows" and "whys" would suggest this. I, for one – but a considerable one – don't believe you were putting it on, giving a woe performance. Perhaps Harpur wouldn't agree, though. He frequently has his own independent thoughts. It's brave, really.'

The police photographers in white overalls and headgear were at the Focus. Judith could see them and Harpur watched her shift a little to the left, trying for a view of Hart now the door of the Ford stood open. Harpur decided she was entitled to this and didn't move to block her attempt. But after a few minutes a body-wagon rolled up and parked between the two cars cutting off completely any sight of the Ford.

Iles said, 'Those blatantly sincere reactions, Judith – did they mean you consider yourself responsible in some way for what happened to him in Cairn Close? Were they an outpouring of self-reproach?'

'In the presence of the dead surely everyone is bound to express feelings of regret, sorrow and loss,' she said.

'Oh, I don't know,' Iles replied.

They saw Judith to her car, just outside the close and then Harpur drove Iles back to headquarters. 'Arc we supposed to believe all that, Col?' Iles said.

'All which, sir?'

'The sentimental luncheon, homage to their past.'

'You think there was something beyond that?'

'Does she strike you as someone who would idolize what's gone and finished? Her interest in Hart would probably die as soon as he'd left school. It was the risk and sauciness of the relationship then that turned her on.'

'I'm not too well up on the psychological side of sex.'

'Hart as lover she's finished with. Hart as private investigator might attract her, though. Perhaps she had a job for him.'

'What job?'

'Of course, she would still have some tender feelings for Hart, and so the noisy grief,' Iles replied. 'She thinks she helped get him killed. Maybe she did.'

Harpur said . . .

EIGHTEEN

B ut there were also times when Harpur didn't say anything at all, and particularly didn't say anything at all to Iles. Generally, this would be a matter of information bagged exclusively by Harpur which he decided should stay exclusive, Iles being the one excluded. It was usually something deeply important, and Iles, as Operations sultan, certainly *should* have been told about it, would rightly *expect* to be told about it, and would *like* to be told about it, if he'd known it existed; which Harpur tried to make sure he didn't. As someone had said, there were things we knew we didn't know; but there were also things we didn't know we didn't know, and this was the kind of multi-aspect ignorance Harpur occasionally managed to stick on Iles, ignorance squared, you could say.

Harpur had one of those precious, concealed items in his mind as they drove back to headquarters from Cairn Close. He'd decided it should stay in his mind for now, just as he'd described to Mrs Groves that Skoda and that Vauxhall as being in Iles's mind, and only in his mind. Useful satchels, minds.

Eternally, Harpur wanted to be a little ahead of Iles; at least a little, possibly more. This was intensely difficult because Iles specialized in aheadness – his – and mercilessly schemed for it. Harpur occasionally wondered whether the assistant chief had been on an advanced personal safety course, perhaps devised originally by Stalin. This taught how to remove permanently anyone who threatened a leader's authority or who *seemed* to threaten a leader's authority; or who appeared likely to consider threatening a leader's authority some time in the future, no matter how far into that future. Insurgency should be put down early, if possible at birth.

Keeping back crucial insights from Iles appeared to Harpur now and then as an extremely appropriate counter-move. He didn't try to define for himself what that appropriateness consisted of. No need, surely. He considered it would have been clunking and fussy. Harpur reckoned he possessed what was termed in the law 'a right to silence', though, admittedly the phrase had a slightly different meaning then. But it required no explanation or excuses. It simply existed, like air, or the sea, or chewing gum, or Mount Kilimanjaro. Of course, he recognized that Iles would continually and ardently suspect Harpur of hiding essential stuff from him. Weren't they both fast-track senior police officers? Iles didn't know it as a certainty, though, lacked details, was carefully denied details, didn't absolutely know he didn't know, could *only* routinely suspect.

What Harpur hid from him for the present was that not long ago, his favourite informant, Jack Lamb, the art dealer, had been in touch with some confidential tip-offs, as he often was, though not lately. Harpur had taken the call at home. Best like that. Frequently, one of his teenage daughters, Hazel or Jill, would get to the receiver first, offer a sham pleasant greeting, listen, and then, without covering the mouthpiece, bellow to Harpur that his tout or nark or stool pigeon or snitch was on the line bubbling with disgusting betrayals, the way touts or narks or stool pigeons or snitches did. This was a kind of joke now. When they'd first done it they'd really meant to show their disapproval. They'd met Jack since then and, to their surprise, liked him. But they kept up the ragging now for the fun of it. Jack tolerated this, more or less.

Harpur and his tout or nark or stool pigeon or snitch would fix a rendezvous where, if there were any bubbling with disgusting betrayals to take place, it might be more secure than on an open landline. Touts, narks, stoolies, snitches had to be careful. Many – most – criminals would like to see them obliterated and turned into *ex* touts, narks, stoolies, snitches, now deceased; perhaps helped along to become deceased, not always painlessly.

'Him, Dad?' Jill, his younger daughter, had asked, when Harpur finished.

'Most probably him,' Hazel, the fifteen-year-old, replied. 'Those very short, nuff-said, probably coded calls, intended to defeat any phone-tap enemies. Squealers have plenty of enemies.' Sometimes Harpur thought they pushed the jape too far.

'Or it could be shame,' Jill said. 'He knows he's a traitor, so get it over fast.'

'Cloak and blabber,' Hazel said.

'Information comes in many different ways,' Harpur replied.

'Some of them pretty nasty,' Hazel said.

'Possibly,' Harpur said. His daughters seemed to believe they had a duty to apply the new generation's values to him, and to monitor his behaviour and attitudes. They'd obviously agreed between them that nobody else would do a proper appraisal job on Harpur, and that he badly needed this proper appraisal. Their mother couldn't help. She was dead, knifed one night in the station car park as she left the late train from London.[4]

Lamb would cite in the brief call an obscure or anonymous meeting place. He and Harpur had agreed three eligible discreet spots which could be rotated. They'd given each a number and only referred to that when fixing a rendezvous. A few nights ago, Jack suggested a one-time anti-aircraft gun site on a hillside at the edge of the city. The concrete emplacements were still there and sittable on. Harpur and Lamb could use a stretch of partly overgrown roadway laid originally for lorries bringing ammunition, food, tea and tit-and-bum magazines in those dark Second World War days. At night as Lamb and he talked, they would gaze down protectively at the massed lights of the buildings and streets and moving traffic. It was a sight German bomber crews would have loved, but all they'd got was blackout, searchlights, hate and ack-ack shells.

For a time the two had abandoned this post because Harpur feared it had become known. But after a while they'd decided the scare was probably wrong and replaced the gun site on their shortlist. Harpur had noticed a special urgency in Lamb's voice when he called that evening to ask for the face-to-face. He had suffered catastrophic trouble recently at the gallery he operated in his country mansion, Darien. Jack's mother, over for a visit from the United States and at ease with pistols, had shot dead a supposed burglar in the gallery and was now in jail.[5] This had badly rocked Jack and his business He hadn't been in contact with Harpur for months and it was a surprise and a relief to hear from him a few days ago.

4 See *Roses, Roses*
5 See *Blaze Away*

Harpur had driven out to the former weapons base and found
Lamb already there, waiting for him, As far as Harpur could see
in the darkness, Jack wore ordinary leisure clothes. Unusual.
Normally, when they met here, Jack would come dressed in gear
from his considerable army surplus collection – bits of British,
German, French Foreign Legion, Russian uniform, or sometimes
a mixture of all four. He did the same when they chose from
their list a defence pill box, built on the foreshore in 1940 to
beat back the Nazi invaders. They never came. Jack adored showy
militariness.

'It's classic isn't it, Colin?' he'd said, almost before Harpur
had climbed out of his car. Lamb's voice seemed ragged now,
more than tense.

'What?'

'First, that awful incident at Darien, and then the spurt of
unrelated results. Or seeming unrelated.'

'What classic unrelated results or classic *seeming* unrelated
results, Jack?'

'That shooting – my mother blazing away in a picture gallery.
This made the papers, made the media generally, didn't it? I
mean on a national scale.'

'Well, yes, it got coverage.'

'It's what they'd call in their glib, trivializing way, a great
story, isn't it – an elderly woman, popping away with a shooter
surrounded by very pricey daubs, noble, historic country house,
an intruder dead, the elderly woman done for manslaughter.'

'Yes, it was going to attract some journalism,' Harpur replied.

'And the effect of that journalism, Colin?' Jack's tone now
was almost plaintive.

'Effect in which sense?'

'In the reputation sense.'

'Whose, Jack – your mother's?'

'To some degree my mother's, yes. Not many people's mothers
kill a stranger in an art gallery. But I don't have to worry much
about *her* reputation. She lives mostly in the States. They might
hear about it over there, and they'll probably think she did well,
guarding the pics and the property and me. A lot of them still
have that holy affection for firearms, and not just to go rabbiting
with. Think of the star, Charlton Heston, fronting for the gun

lobby. "Every citizen has a constitutional right to shoot another citizen's head off if that other citizen looks dangerous, or might get to look dangerous any time shortly, unless his head is blasted off now.'"

'So, when you say reputation you mean your own, do you, Jack?'

'I mean the Darien gallery's, and my own, yes. We co-exist. We cohere. Great art is sniffy about the company it keeps, and the settings it's in.'

'How can all that harm you and the gallery?' Harpur said. 'You didn't do the shooting. As I remember it, you cooperated with the police.'

'I did, I did – talking to your colleague Garland and others. But there are people in London and Manchester and Paris and Cairo and Antwerp and Ghent who'll get reports of the disaster, and how will they respond, Colin?'

'That's a tricky one, Jack.'

'No, it isn't. Not if you know this trade. They'll say: "That sounds like a dodgy type of gallery and business. It has a shoot-to-kill old lady on the premises. Had." They'll start to think greedily about Darien – how they can make something of it for themselves now its position is sure to be shaky. They'll wonder whether the Darien owner – "moniker Jack Lamb, is it?" – they'll ask themselves whether this Jack Lamb can survive the appalling, farcical havoc, police and press acting very intrusive. There'll be the smell of cordite over Darien. There'll be a drop in trustworthiness. There'll be the lawyer's bill for getting his mother's murder charge reduced. There'll be a long, possibly bankrupting break from normal dealing. This is a situation that some of them will decide is worth looking into, don't you think, Colin? Jack Lamb will appear weak, forced to flog off works cheap, a fire sale, if he's to keep the business running. Bargains! Snips!'

'You speculate this, do you, Jack? It hasn't actually happened?'

Lamb had been pacing about among the imagined artillery, now and then staring up into the black sky, as though to home in on a Dornier that could be blasted. Probably from watching a state funeral on TV he'd learned how to do the army slow march – one respectful half step forward, pause, then the other

half – and he'd been practising that. He stopped. Harpur had
sat down on the low surrounding wall of the guns position and
Lamb stood unmoving now in front of him. Jack was 6' 5" and
about 260 lbs, He blocked Harpur's view of the city. Harpur
had sensed that what might be coming next from Lamb could
be crucial. And it would be delivered downwards at him from
this looming, mighty physique. It was like being addressed by
a wall.

Tonight's get-together didn't match the usual tout, nark, stool
pigeon, snitch session, with Jack passing on selected information
about crimes or intended crimes that he felt to be particularly
odious and anti-social. Jack wasn't simply an observer of the
villainy or potential villainy now. He'd become part of it. He
was encompassed. He wanted help.

'I've had approaches. Why I asked for the meeting,' he said.

'Approaches?'

'All right, *an* approach. There'll be others, though. I know it.'

'An approach how, Jack?'

'Direct.'

'Direct in which way?'

'Direct in a direct way.'

'Meaning?'

Lamb paused, as though what he would reveal now might
seem incredible and therefore should get a measured, unmelo-
dramatic mention. He said, 'One of them arrived in a van with
a wheeled suitcase, a capacious wheeled suitcase, full of cash,
and spoke of an interest in two particular modern works. He'd
been very accurately briefed, Colin, on what pictures I had here,
on the walls or in the cellar lock-away. Some good, professional
research had been done. It's disturbing.'

'You saw the money?'

'Higgledy-piggledy, amassed in an excited rush, not neat,
rubber-banded packs, but very genuine looking, tens, twenties,
fifties. Somebody was in a hurry, wanted to get in first with the
offer, no time for tidiness.'

'Did you know him?'

'He wasn't a main man,' Lamb said.

'Someone handling a deal for someone else?'

'Someone *hoping* to handle a deal for someone else,' Lamb

replied. 'Someone hoping to handle a deal for someone else who's large scale and flush with crook cash he or she wants turned into something respectable and reeking of culture?'

'Laundering,' Harpur said.

'Why I said classic,' Lamb replied. 'Commonplace. Isn't it? Investment in art. It's a standard ploy for dumping ill-gotten loot – drugs cash especially, but also, protection cash, robbery cash, fraud cash, kidnap cash, terrorist cash, menaces cash. These days, pictures are international currency, but safer, and not subject to exchange rates. Dirty money gets cleaned up, made impeccable. And more than that, it can be transformed into something gloriously distinguished. Then, after a decent, tactical gap, the purchases will be sold on, alchemized into cash again, but now cash from an apparently above-board, honest bit of trading. It's called "the Balkan strategy". Don't know why.

'The new rich tend to go for contemporary pieces, not the ancients, so launderers buy modern, knowing they can get a fine price for it at an eventual re-sell. Take a look at auction prices reached in GB, China, Japan, the US for, say, works by Jeff Koons, or Warhol, or Hoyland or Twombly or Emin or Hirst, or Ligon or Ofili. They will give you an idea of the going rates. Of course, most sales are totally fine and legal. A few, no.'

'The assistant launderer gave a name – his own or his employer's?' Harpur replied.

'He said to call him Monsieur Rendrecompte. Mr Invoice. This is above all a merchantile situation, not to do with aesthetics. Colin.'

'He was French? Belgian?'

'The word was French. But I'd say his accent seemed Brit, even local.'

'You didn't know him, recognize him, though?'

'I can give you a description, Colin.'

'You refused the suitcase offer, did you?'

'Of course, I fucking did. OK, I don't want to get prim. As we know, there are disreputable areas to some art trading, and it's true that I might, accidentally, have been involved in such business now and then. Inadvertently.'

'Accidentally?' Harpur said.

'Accidentally. Utterly accidentally.'

'Right, utterly accidentally,' Harpur replied. 'Utterly, utterly accidentally. Inadvertently.'

Lamb said, 'We don't always know the full provenance of a picture or sculpture, and this can draw a dealer into dubious territory. As I believe some US statesman said, we know there are things we don't know but there are also things we don't know we don't know.'

'Fascinating,' Harpur replied.

'But M. Rendrecompte's laundering mission was so crude, so screamingly blatant, so much a cliché, that hardly any dealer would look at it.'

'Did you part friends?' Harpur had asked.

'Do I want friends like that?'

Do you want enemies like that, or like whoever it was that sent him with the money on luggage castors? He/she might feel disrespected, and vengeful. But Harpur hadn't said this, only added it to those other unsaids in his mind, that mute pandemonium.

'I just thought you ought to know the situation, Colin.' Lamb had been preparing to leave.

'Well, yes, thanks, Jack.'

'On the face of it, I suppose no offence has been committed. We don't know the money was bad money. It was, of course, but I can see it might be hard to prove.'

'More of that slipperiness in the word "know". I'll keep an eye,' Harpur replied.

'That's all I'd hope for, Colin.'

Most likely it wasn't, but Jack would find it humiliating to ask for better defined help. He'd probably expect Harpur to pick up the unspoken signals and do something about them. Harpur *did* pick up the unspoken signals. He didn't see what he could do about them though.

As he and Iles drove back to headquarters from the body in the Ford Focus at Cairn Close, all these factors jostled spikily and separately in his head, but he found that his brain, more or less of itself, with no conscious prompting from the brain's proprietor, was trying to synthesize this awkward lot, bring it into some kind of unity and sense and recognizable shape. His reason wanted to shepherd in together Lamb's boodle bearing visitor, and the blasted Focus in Cairn with Hart sprawled, resprawled, over the wheel. Where the fuck was the connection, though? The only connection was Harpur: he'd heard of or seen both. But surely it amounted to a kind of daft egomania to imagine this proved a link between the art courier and Thomas Wells Hart in the Focus, didn't it? His brain could produce the questions OK, not the answers. He had no QED. Darien was Darien with all its woes, and Cairn was the close with its purged-pockets deado.

They were drawing in to the yard at headquarters. Iles said, 'Judith Vasonne comes to spend a little holiday break with her sister-in-law and brother on our patch while hubby is occupied elsewhere. That's credible. Presumably she has no kids. While with her relatives she gets in touch with a one-time boy lover. No, I don't believe that was a revival of old sexual interests. Youth is no longer her taste. But this particular one-time youth is now a private detective, and apparently very good at it. She might have still been at the school when he got the job with Bainbridge and knew about it; might even have heard he'd quickly earned a partnership, has exceptional talent, and not just shagwise. Is that why she contacts him again, Col?'

'You think so, sir?' Iles could often bring off almost mystical and telepathic glimpses like this.

'What has she seen at the sister-in-law and brother's house that causes her to ring Tom Hart?' the ACC asked.

'What *has* she seen, sir?'

'This I don't know. That might sound like a dim and negligent condition to be in. Wrong. *Because* I know I don't know, and because this is not an unknown unknown, I can feel, *do* feel, I ought to and will correct the not knowing that I know about by finding out what it is I at present don't know. The not knowing can be remedied because the not knowing is not unknown. Then I will know that I know. This is what it means to be Operations in brackets, Col.'

'I know,' Harpur replied.

NINETEEN

Of course, I didn't find out about that meeting between Harpur and Jack Lamb until later on, and then only through hints. But never mind about the meeting; I'd actually witnessed what Lamb described to Harpur – the arrival of the blue van and its driver.

We'll get to that shortly. There is some other material to fit in first.

I don't think Judith could have read in my face that I thought her bugging notion a probable non-starter; a more than probable non-starter. I certainly didn't say this to her. It would have made her feel snubbed, or worse: naïve, clumsy, stupid. I dreaded the idea of hurting her in any way. After all, hadn't she been part of my education, and not just in Religious Studies? Especially not in Religious Studies. I owed Judith plenty. She'd saved me from feet. Much of what I knew about women came from Judith. It helped me now and then, for instance, with Irene Celadon, the 'someone else' Judy wanted to ask about at The Knoll, but didn't; probably couldn't, because she'd decided my sex life was the past and therefore of no concern to her any longer – except that it obviously and confidentially was.

But I said she shouldn't secretly unlock any doors at her brother and sister-in-law's house, Failsafe, quite yet, and that, first, I'd do some general inquiries. I could tell this disappointed her; more than disappointed her: riled her. Maybe she feared it was my rotten way of side-stepping her scheme. OK, perhaps she'd be part right. God, the sliminess and falsity of 'quite yet', words pretending to be nicely judged and gradual, but really meaning, 'for fuck's sake stuff the bug guff, Judy'.

'Exactly what general inquiries, Tom?' she'd asked.

'Preparatory.'

'To what?'

'I'd need to look into the art situation mentioned by your sister-in-law.'

'The bugging could do that for you. It would be background to the Failsafe meetings and discussions.'

'*Might* be. We've no clear notion of what his business is, have we? I'd like to dig into that.'

'This is what I mean,' she'd answered. 'The bugging would tell us.'

'Possibly. I'd prefer the more roundabout way of coming at it. For now. "Softly, softly, catchee monkey."'

'Bollocks,' she replied.

Yes, it was: a hack proverb to help me skip commitment. For a few seconds I thought Judy would go on with the argument, but then she seemed to accept that, whatever she said, I'd use my own methods: the methods I'd been trained in. This wasn't school days any longer. Perhaps I wished it was. She shelved the bugging idea, and our meal at The Knoll had finished amiably enough: a bit of cheek-kissing, checks we hadn't changed mobile numbers, and promises to keep in touch.

My intention was still to help her – in genuine honour of how we had been for each other way back. I'd do it, though, by proving Judith's worry about her brother's work was nuts. I had a positive aim: to negative suspicion. The proof would need to be clear and real. Judith had a brain. She'd spot any make-believe and lies. I'd have to be very skilful, and very invisible, especially at the start. I must stay unseen, or I'd be snookered, whether he had anything to hide or not. If Judith found I'd been exposed she'd naturally assume that Keith and his associates would change their behaviour for a while, go harmless and respectable, supposing the behaviour had previously been bad – crooked, criminal. There'd be no hope of finding the truth.

Or, suppose they were innocent – which I thought likely – they'd carry on being innocent, regardless of a spy, me. There'd be nothing worthwhile for a spy – me – to spy on. But if they *were* into villainy they'd do that super cover-up and switch, temporarily at least, to a strong, thorough show of innocence for the spy – me – and any other spy colleagues.

I drove out towards Rastelle Major to take a look at the Vasonne property, Failsafe. I already had an idea of the layout from Judith's drawing, and a Google visit, but I wanted to see the actual building and grounds in their setting. This – the setting, the geography

– was crucial. It would dictate the kind of secret observation possible, or not. Yes, or not. That private eye course listed the indispensable conditions for concealed surveillance. We were told not to try it unless all of these were in place, repeat, all.

It was a fairly modern, large, detached double-fronted property, five bedrooms, several bathrooms, straggling ivy up the facade over the front porch, a separate brick double garage, I thought I could make out the side door into the so-said so buggable conference room that Judith had spoken about. There was nobody coming to or going from that garden door while I watched. A concrete path leading to a gate on to the road split the front lawn into two. The rear garden had a pool, a children's chute and climbing frame and a gazebo.

Failsafe was one of three similar detached houses built on the edge of a small copse. The Internet gave the most recent purchase price, presumably by the Vasonnes, as £950,000. Three sources formed my summing-up of the spread: Judith's sketch; the Internet; and now, personal viewing. The last was easily the weakest. A secret snoop would be impossible, either on foot or in the car. The three houses stood in a little line off the road. It wouldn't get much traffic and what there was could be easily seen from one of the bay windows; similarly, any pedestrian hanging about. It would be stupid for me to dawdle here. I stopped for a couple of minutes in the car, did my quick bit of useless gazing at the gazebo etcetera, then pushed on towards Rastelle Major.

Well, for a mile or two towards Rastelle Major. I decided, though, on a second residence inspection, but now a different one mentioned by Judith: Jack Lamb's Darien. This should be easier. I'd passed Darien several times when driving to see clients of the firm who lived out that way. The house lay in a hollow. On one side of it was a hillock where ash, beech and willows grew: Chase Woods. I could watch from there without being obvious. I wouldn't be very close but I always carried field glasses in the car.

I'd Googled Darien, too. A caption to the photographs said parts of it dated back nearly five hundred years, though there'd been subsequent changes and additions. The note also suggested that the name, Darien, a region of Panama, had probably been taken from a Keats sonnet, and if so couldn't be as old as the house. In the seventeenth-century Civil War it was a Royalist stronghold and there'd been local skirmishes. There'd been a local skirmish more recently, too: Jack Lamb's mother with a handgun saw to that.

I took a narrow B road route up towards Chase Woods, left the car in a layby and walked to a spot from where I could see everything except the far side of the house, while pretty well concealed by the trees and bushes. There were flagstone terraces at the front and back, a circular swimming pool, and several outbuildings, including what could be staff bungalows, a summer house, stables and a couple of barns, perhaps used as garages now. Art could supply a nice living for some.

Not much moved. A middle-aged woman came out briefly from a side door, lit a cigarette and had half a dozen quick, deep drags. When she'd finished she bent and thoroughly ground out the stub. She seemed to push the remnant through a drain cover under one of the down pipes, then went back in to what was probably the kitchen.

The furtive, fervent beat-the-ban smoking session had distracted me. When I put the glasses back on to the front, tree-lined, gravelled drive, I saw a small blue van approaching the house. It stopped near the porch. The driver climbed swiftly out and went to the rear of the vehicle. He opened the doors and produced a large, grey and black-wheeled suitcase. He carried this on to the terrace and could then use the wheels. When he had the case in his arms he held it with what seemed a loving reverence, as though the most precious item in some outlawed religious ritual. He made for Darien's main entrance, and went out of sight in the brick-walled porch. I guessed he'd been admitted to the house. A salesman of some sort, with his samples in the case? Wasn't there a collection of poems called A Case of Samples. Clairvoyant?

I didn't recognize the man. He'd be about forty. He wore a dark-blue, double-breasted, buttoned-up, three-piece suit, collar and tie, no hat, black shoes. He had what looked to me a full head of fair hair worn quite long. There was a kind of dogged-ness to his movements around the van and then on to the terrace. As far as I could make out, the vehicle had no lettering on the body, nothing to tell me what this visitor's trade might be. Even

with the field glasses I was too far away to be certain of the
registration number. I believed I could distinguish a T and an L
and a figure 6: but very maybe.

I imagined I might have a long wait if there was a lot of stuff
in the case to be displayed and talked up. His formal clothes
suggested he dealt in serious, expensive goods. In fact, though,
he reappeared from the porch after only four or five minutes.
Some of that doggedness seemed to have gone. He pushed the
case on its castors ahead of him. His head was half turned back,
as if he were talking to someone or listening. I saw a tenseness
about him now, his thin frame crouched over the extended handle
to the case.

A tall, heavily-made, middle-aged man in shirt sleeves and
khaki, calf-length, *Bridge on the River Kwai* shorts took a few
steps out from the porch after the newcomer and appeared to say
something to him. I assumed this second man must be Jack Lamb.
I'd never met him but had heard about Lamb, of course, at the
time of the Darien gallery shooting. He watched while the stranger
returned to the van and put the case into the back. He moved
around to open the driver's door. Before he got in he stood facing
Lamb and seemed to stare at him for several seconds then shook
his head a couple of times as if in disbelief or regret. Or threat?
He climbed into the van, did a three-point turn and left. Lamb
stared after the vehicle until it must have cleared the grounds: I
couldn't see that far because of trees bordering the drive.

Lamb went back into the house. I decided I'd just watched
someone being kicked off the property, regardless of whether he
smoked. And what about the suitcase, then? It had seemed central
to this little episode, but I'd no notion what was in it. At least,
I'd no notion what was in it when the episode began. I'd wondered,
hadn't I, about samples: van man trying some doorstepping on
a grand, historic manor house scale?

I began to doubt this. Could that loving embrace of the case
signify not a spiritual, sacred item but an all-powerful, irresistible, very tangible force? In other words, I thought cash. And,
thinking of cash, my mind went back somehow to what Judith
had spoken about at The Knoll. Well, no, it wasn't just 'somehow'.
I could trace a definite sequence. She was perturbed in case her
brother had been drawn into shady, cheapo art dealing at Darien

following the gallery shoot-out. Was I wrong to dismiss her worries? Had I just watched a big-timer – or a courier for a big-timer – bring luggaged money to trade with in a discount market? Had Jack Lamb ejected him because it wasn't enough; amounted to an insult even in cut-price circumstances?

Or there could be some other reason: possibly Lamb saw he had been chosen to provide a loot laundering service via art, so fashionable among new-age hoodlums, and refused this invitation as too risky. I wished I'd asked Judith for a description of her brother. Did he favour sombre, waist-coated suits? Did he keep his fair hair long? Did he do stare sessions aimed at scaring whoever got one of them?

I returned through the wood to my car and drove down the hill a little way and turned left, so I would pass the entrance to the Darien grounds. The Google remarks about the house had also mentioned that in the style of the period when the mansion was built a stone tablet had been fixed to one of the main gates bearing a Latin inscription. It had survived through the centuries. The words came from Horace and said: *Omnes Eodem Cogimur*, (We are all herded to the same place).

And there it still was. I wondered why the succession of occupants must have bothered to look after for centuries such a thumping slice of triteness. Answer: 'Yea, but it's Latin triteness.' Just the same, not many people were herded into a splendid manor house like Darien as their home. And at least one who turned up there with his venerated, loaded suitcase was apparently told to fuck off back to wherever pronto. I drove on. Timewise, of course, I was driving on towards that very rough bit of rough house at Cairn Close and my subsequent, notable funeral.

TWENTY

Harpur said – and he's entitled to some wordage now, perhaps – 'The Hart funeral, sir?' He and Iles were talking in Harpur's room at headquarters, the ACC looking out of a window on to the busy afternoon city scene, probably feeling solely responsible for everyone's safety, and glad to feel responsible for it. He'd be thinking the populace didn't know how lucky they were to have him. Iles would have been very unwilling to tell them for fear of seeming a braggart; but he'd seethe that they didn't spot it spontaneously. 'The coroner has released the body,' Harpur said.

'I shall go to the service, of course, Col,' Iles replied.

This Harpur had expected, though he'd idiotically hoped to hear the opposite. Iles had form at funerals. If he attended one, Harpur had to go, also, in case the assistant chief needed restraining at some crux point. Because Iles decided for himself, in his own super-cryptic style, what *were* crux points, Harpur had to be non-stop vigilant.

No police training course covered how to reduce an ACC to harmlessness in a place of worship or crematorium chapel, and Harpur had been forced to work out a method for himself. He had made notes of successful tactics during previous disturbances and he kept the file headed 'Observations On Religion Sited Obsequies' in his triple-locked safe at headquarters. Harpur's wife, Megan, used to have a volume called *The Rules and Exercises of Holy Dying* on the shelves at home, but she had died in deeply unholy conditions and her library was taken away except for two titles Jill wanted kept, a book on boxing, *The Sweet Science,* and *The Joe Orton Diaries.* It was customary for a senior officer to attend the funeral of innocent victims of crime, to show sympathy and demonstrate that police had this death in mind.

Meaning well, and missing it by a fucking country mile, the ACC would sometimes try to take over the service. A coffin really gingered him up, regardless of quality, valid timber or cardboard. Several times he'd explained to Harpur that he totally and absolutely loathed discrimination, except where it was useful. He liked to give certain funerals a personal slant, his, rather than the corpse's. Harpur believed that to Iles this seemed a duty: the funeral would be a lesser funeral without his pro-active management; scarcely a funeral at all, in fact. He would see only shortcomings and skimping in the way the thing was being run before his kindly, reassuring intervention. Aura was what he found some funerals short of, and he would try to remedy this deficit by supplying plentiful aura of his own. He probably believed he had so much he could easily afford to dole some around. He'd always be superbly dressed and coiffured for the ceremony. He had told Harpur he felt he owed a first-class, faultless appearance to the congregation, no matter what a crowd of oiks and shitbags they might preponderantly be. When perfectly turned out he felt he lent – unstintingly lent – yes, lent a distinction to the event, and therefore to the ex.

He craved prominence, for himself and for his special spiel of the day. Once he had successfully beaten off opposition and entrenched himself in a pulpit it could be very difficult removing the assistant chief, particularly if the pulpit were up steps. In Anglican churches and cathedrals many were. Iles would trick or scare or manhandle the proper occupant out, and so gain a position reasonably simple to defend, just as the hilltop abbey at Monte Cassino had been in the Second World War, apparently. Iles could punch or kick down at a vicar or priest or undertaker or Harpur attempting to retake the fastness, and/or unhook a microphone, if there was one fitted there, and use this as a knobkerrie.

Obviously, it would be highly untoward for Harpur to come to a funeral wearing a helmet and/or body armour and Iles knew this, deftly exploited it. Although some of these unconventional interludes certainly brought a vigour and passion to what might otherwise have been a dreary religious rigmarole, on the whole Harpur felt the scrapping lacked dignity and was very untidy. Weddings often produced violence among the guests, yes, but Harpur thought it definitely inappropriate for funerals. Admittedly, the mayhem proved the presence of life in the mourners, as

against the nicely behaved stillness of death in the box. But
Harpur would argue that there were more suitable ways of high-
lighting this important difference.

The shoes Iles used in his attempt to kick unconscious anyone
on the steps impertinently trying to get at him were undoubtedly
the magnificent, custom-made Charles Laity black lace-ups
costing hundreds, but, even so, Harpur considered this could not
make the ACC's behaviour any more dainty. To somebody getting
an Iles toe-cap in the face, given added force by its downward
trajectory and possibly breaking a nose or cheekbone, this would
rate simply as a shoe, its special qualities and position in the
footwear league table, irrelevant; not that the Laity firm advertised
the shoes as designed for this kind of unfriendly exchange,
anyway, whether lace-up or slip-on.

Naturally, the assistant chief's careful smartness would be
undone if Harpur had to grab a handful of his hair to drag him
from a pulpit, usually down the steps, though occasionally over
the side of it, his exquisitely shod feet threshing in the air now
and perhaps knocking a big, hardback Bible from its perch, with
obvious risk to the binding. Harpur would try to get Iles into a
neutral aisle and struggle to hold him there, though humanely
guarding against stoppage of air to his lungs. This pause would
allow the priest, or whatever, to regain control and proceed to
the eulogies. Blood on the fine material of the ACC's dress
uniform would come out OK at the cleaners but it didn't look
good during the actual rites. However, Harpur did judge it very
creditable that although Iles might yell and froth a lot when
delivering his commentary in this kind of melee, he hardly ever
swore much. Never at a funeral, as far as Harpur could recall,
had Iles howled the worst curse words. He'd declared that to do
so would be unforgivably disrespectful, not just to the dead
person, of whichever gender or none, but to decorum and religion
in general 'throughout what we must now refer to, Col, as "the
global village"', meaning everywhere.' Iles was a firm fan of
decorum, though he did take breaks.

TWENTY-ONE

Omnes Eodem Cogimur. (We are all herded to the same place.)
About three miles along the road from Darien's gates I spotted the blue van a few hundred yards ahead of me, stopped in a layby. A black Audi saloon was parked very tightly in at its tail. There appeared to be nobody in the car. From behind I couldn't see whether the front seat, seats, of the van were occupied.

I cut my speed, though not too noticeably, I hoped. I wasn't sure how to cope. Should I drive past, observing as much as I could, including the reg numbers of both vehicles? Or should I choose to get herded by luck and opportunity into the same place as the two vehicles and perhaps meet some of their personnel and try to work out what their game was? I might credibly be a driver in need of a few minutes to make a mobile phone call; or for a pee-pause behind one of the bushes alongside the layby.

I decided it would be timorous and pathetically negative to keep going. And unprofessional: that private dick course had preached the towering importance of what were called 'sudden breakthrough moments' – the need to recognize them quickly, and get what could be got from them. There might be a double bounty here: two vehicles, one of which I knew to be part of that baffling encounter at Darien, and the other apparently involved in a layby rendezvous, most likely pre-arranged. I pulled in and switched off, I didn't copy the Audi and get in close but left a decent gap, so as not to seem aggressive or half-witted or both. I stayed in my car for a while. Nothing changed.

I climbed out and took cover among the foliage for a genuine piss with genuine male, from-a-height splash sounds: authentic detail in this kind of ploy was crucial. When I returned to the Focus I found a dumpy, fair-skinned woman in her twenties, mousy hair top-knotted, denim jacket, khaki chinos trousers, blue and white plimsolls, standing near the driver's door and looking away down the road, perhaps to save me from embarrassment.

Tact. I checked my zip. 'Hello,' I said, 'anything wrong here or hereabouts?'

She turned towards me and gave a really thorough, expertly prepared smile, taking a good half of her face, possibly more like two thirds, and lasting four or five seconds. 'I don't think we've met before,' she replied, her voice warm and wistful, as if touched by regret that we'd negligently let so much time pass with no contact. 'Certainly, we haven't previously run across each other in this type of situation,' she added.

'Which?'

'Is that your impression, too?'

'Of what?'

'Not having already met.'

'That's the thing about laybys,' I replied.

'What?'

'No knowing who'll be in one. Or whether anyone at all will be there. Laybys have no settled agenda. It's not like booking a couple of orchestra stalls for *The Flying Dutchman*.'

'You seem to know a lot about them.'

'I haven't made a systematic Phd study. It's just what I've noticed. Some have an information board saying they *are* laybys, but with others the drivers have to work it out for themselves, using instinct and experience. I reckon that's reasonable enough. If there's a convenient but limited area just off the road what else could it be but a layby.'

'I wonder whether we're on your usual route,' she replied.

'I have a choice. I can take this road or a couple of others. The destination would be the same. "We are all herded to the same place," as someone said.'

'Horace. And if you ask me "Horace Who?" I'll throw up.'

'A lot of these people come out with sayings,' I replied. 'If they didn't produce such chewy snippets we'd most probably never have heard of them.'

'Which people?'

'Horace's sort. He's most likely a good way back in history.'

'BC.'

'There you are then. Yet his ideas are still with us. That's how he is remembered, despite the centuries.'

'Odes.'

'Exactly. We all have thoughts, but with someone like Horace a thought arrives and he gives a little whoop, or whatever they did BC when deliciously surprised, and decides immediately that this has Ode qualities. Probably friends look in on him and ask, "Any new Odes for us, Hor?" and he wouldn't want to let them down.'

'Where are you making for?' she said. 'Just out of curiosity.'

'This general forward direction. I'm a believer in that.'

'What?'

'Going to where the front of the car seems to be pointing. How about you?'

'What I'm getting at,' she replied, 'is, if you're near wherever it is you're going, it would seem odd to have to delay here.'

'I'll push on shortly,' I replied. 'You too? Are you with the van or the Audi?'

'That interests you, does it?' she replied.

'I see two vehicles so I have to assume two drivers, plus possible passengers,' I said. 'There's nobody in the Audi. I'm going to deduce, therefore, that *you* drove that one but have left it momentarily, and so are available to come and discuss matters with me. This would obviously mean the Audi is temporarily empty. The van? There must be at least one person in the cab – the driver – but he hasn't appeared.'

'It does interest you, does it?'

'I take it these two vehicles are a unit in some way,' I replied. 'The calculated nearness.'

'How do you mean "in some way"?' she said.

'Yes, in some way. This I would maintain is a reasonable deduction. The calculated nearness. The extreme proximity. Anyone who viewed the positioning of those two vehicles would suppose a connection.'

'Is that why you decided to pop into the layby?'

'Why would two vehicles with very considerable togetherness cause me to, as you put it, "pop into the layby"?' I said with a gentle, ribbing type of chuckle.

'Yes, why would they?' she asked.

'We agreed early on that we'd probably never met before,' I replied. 'I'd certainly remember any previous conversation of this rather disjointed, anti-linear nature. I expect you'd agree. Are you concerned with art at all? I don't mean, necessarily, are you a painter or sculptor, but having to do with art in some quite meaningful fashion. This is a notion that jumped into my head from who knows where when I first saw you near the Focus just now? Random. Unexpected.'

'Which of the two vehicles interests you more?' she replied. 'As I imagine it, you're driving along, the front of your Focus, as you said, pointing in the direction you're going, and suddenly notice the car and the van in the layby and you exclaim to yourself silently or even, perhaps, aloud, "Hello, there's an Audi in the layby, not a vehicle I recognize." I put that one first because it would be the nearest to you as your Focus approached. But it might easily have been, instead, "Hello, there's a blue van in the layby, not a vehicle I recognize." And another possibility, of course, is, "Hello, there's an Audi and a van in the layby, not vehicles I recognize." Which of these might it have been? Can you recall?'

'Your questions seem to suggest that I probably know very well not simply laybys in general but this layby particularly, and would therefore be alert to any unusual visitors there,' I replied.

'I wouldn't say "unusual".'

'Few would see an inevitable oneness between a blue van and an Audi.'

'But you did, did you?' she said.

'Is there a colleague in the van?'

'We've discussed where you might be going *to*, but just as significant might be where you were coming *from*,' she replied.

'If there's someone in the van he might be wondering why you are such a long while talking to a Ford Focus driver,' I said. 'Might he come to join us, d'you think, out of puzzlement or to appear sociable. Is he in touch with art, also?'

'Why do you say "he"? You've said "he" four times. Have you seen the blue van before – that is, the blue van and its driver?'

'Where *could* I have seen it?'

'Yes, where?' she said.

'I don't maintain that because the van and the Audi are so near each other some transference operation might be taking place, or has taken place, like a plane refuelling another in mid-air.

There is no evidence of that. In any case, such a transference of an item or items would be easier if the Audi were backed up to the van, not head-on to it. The very adjacent vehicles do seem to imply some kind of shared purpose, but not necessarily a shifting of load from one to the other. Would you accept this as a fair summary?'

'You mention "no evidence",' she said. 'Are you police? A detective? That's their kind of lingo, though they can sometimes *concoct* evidence, I gather, so that where there was no evidence there now *is* evidence, evidence, fortunately, of just the brand they want because they created it.'

'I saw no loading from the van to the Audi or vice versa.'

'What kind of loading didn't you see?' she said.

'Loads can certainly vary.'

'Could you give me some examples?'

'The van is small,' I replied, 'but it could accommodate quite a significant amount of items if required to, or several large items. It's well known that some small vans have a surprising amount of capacity despite the left and right casements for the rear wheels taking some of the space. Have you thought, though, that if a police patrol car comes this way on a routine drive through local streets and roads the officers might regard the nearness of the Audi to the van as something of a mystery and come to have a nose around. I'm not hinting that there's something criminal about the closeness, but it's odd. The patrol might decide to investigate.'

'I'll be on my way soon,' she said.

'Ah. It's been a very pleasant interlude. I take it you'll be driving the Audi, yes? Will you and the van part together?'

'There's no real reason for me to stay. It was just that I wondered why you'd come to the layby, whether there was more to it than bladder pressure.'

'That's very understandable. I'm so happy we were able to have a constructive discussion on this topic and I hope I've explained everything with total clarity.'

'Not at all, you devious, jabbering shite,' she said. 'Did you mention "disjointed"? I'd say all over the place.'

'The same place as we're all being herded to?'

I drove out of the layby, passing the two vehicles and managed an excellent stare into the van's side window. Suitcase Man was sitting at the wheel gazing ahead and seemed to ignore the Focus. Should there be a profile resemblance to Judy? Couldn't see one. I felt proud and exceptionally mature to have earned that farewell chirp from the Audi piece, 'jabbering, devious shite'. It showed she hadn't been able to get much from our quaint, roadside gossip.

TWENTY-TWO

Harpur was upstairs at 126 Arthur Street carefully getting himself ready for Thomas Wells Hart's funeral: essential to ensure every detail right and respectful. Dignity, above all, was what he wanted for the service, and he knew he must do what he could to contribute some of that dignity. He wore a good, dark, double-breasted three-piece suit on these occasions: off-the-peg, a long-term joke to Iles, but expensive by Harpur's standards, the shoulder pads unboxy, the lapels unspivvy, and the jacket with quite decently deep, pockets. Methodically, he put a knuckleduster into one of these and a pair of handcuffs in the other. These were additional measures that might be needed if Iles grew emotional and unduly showy at funerals. Harpur would never think of tasering an assistant chief constable (Operations) though. The finger irons and cuffs had to be enough. The shop assistant at Marks and Spencer where Harpur bought the suit seemed baffled by his fussiness over pocket depths.

Harpur didn't rigidly designate one side or the other of his jacket pockets for each of these accessories: say, the knuckleduster required always to go to the right, the handcuffs to the left, or vice versa. Difficulties sourced by Iles might come from any direction and in unpredictable waves, like a disturbed bee swarm, and in almost any form, making it impossible to know in advance which of Harpur's special funeral aids would be the more appropriate. He sought a general, ready, all-round usefulness from them. No more than that could be spelled out. If he were forced to attempt a forecast of how things might go, he'd say the irons to stop Iles, the handcuffs to secure and slowly neutralize him, somewhere out of sight and, if possible, out of hearing of the funeral party and clergy, because of possible heated language – though no cursing – in pleas, protests, denunciations from a manacled assistant chief (Ops.) This version of possible incidents was a guess only, no absolutes. Vestries could be ideal accommodation for Iles when recovering from one of his spasms, especially in ancient churches where the vestry might have a very heavy oak door, lockable from outside. As an additional precaution, the manacle from one wrist could be fixed to the handle of something cumbersome and difficult to drag around such as a nice sized box of spare knee cushions.

It was the school holidays and his daughters were elsewhere in the house or out in the garden. The front doorbell rang. Harpur always preferred to answer it himself. His daughters would allow almost anyone in and as a rule get a nosy conversation going with the visitor, visitors, immediately, for instance, an exchange of information about family trees and/or a mutual listing of favourite lettuce types. Harpur thought he might be able to get to the front door ahead of Hazel and Jill, particularly if they were in the garden.

He hurriedly took the knuckledusters and handcuffs out of his pockets and put them in Denise's dressing table knickers drawer. Denise, his occasional live-in, undergraduate girlfriend, had gone home to see her parents in Stafford during the vacation. Harpur knew she had other knickers. He knew, also, that if Jill noticed the bulges in his jacket pockets, and she would, she'd want to discover what caused this – was he carrying what she'd learned from TV cop dramas to call a piece – even two pieces – meaning a handgun, or handguns. Harpur had hoped to slip away to the funeral without doing more than give a quick 'see you later' to his daughters. Matters might be more long drawn out and talkative now.

Jill didn't have any strong views either way about police carrying guns, but she would assume that if he had one aboard, or even two, he must be going somewhere serious, dangerous. That she did object to. Today, there was no gun, but she might be able to work out from the shapes what he was carrying, and he didn't want to signal that the assistant chief could turn inchoate now and then and had to be catered for, though he *could* turn inchoate now and then, and they probably already knew it.

He'd got out on to the landing on his way to the stairs when he heard and saw the door open and Jill seeming to welcome someone. Then the door was shut. Jill shouted, 'For you, Dad. A lady. She wants to talk to you personal.'

'Personally,' Harpur said, reaching the bottom of the stairs.

'That as well. A Mrs Gaston.'

Harpur saw a woman of about sixty. She had on a beige cardigan, over a white blouse, and a cream knee-length skirt. Harpur thought he might have glimpsed her somewhere previously, but couldn't remember where or when.

'Dad's going to a funeral. A murder in Cairn Close. You might of heard of it,' Jill said.

'*Have* heard of it,' Harpur said.

'Well, of course, you would of heard of it. You're the police,' Jill replied.

'Not "of heard of it".'

'Why not?' Jill replied.

'Oh, God,' Hazel said.

'Volleys. No messing,' Jill said. 'Officers go to this kind of funeral for what's called "community closeness". Sympathy and so on. Dad's an officer, a chief super, although he doesn't wear a uniform because of being a detective. They go in plain clothes so they can mingle and not be obvious before they make their pounce. You'll notice his special funeral suit. But he'll have time for a brief chat. He's always ready to talk to callers.'

'It's about the funeral that I wanted to speak,' Mrs Gaston said.

'People often come to see him,' Jill replied. 'They can get his address from the phone book or on line. Not all police have their numbers in the directories. It might bring trouble from villains, such as windows broken or rude graffiti on the house front. I've been told people used to regard most cops as OK. Not now.'

'Good thing, too,' Hazel said.

'Haze's view of all that is a bit sour because one of the topmost police here, Assistant Chief Desmond Iles, really fancied her way back although underage and Mr Iles had a wife. That's Haze underage, not him, naturally. He's Dad's boss,' Jill said. 'He's got a crimson scarf which he wore loose, not tucked in anywhere, so he could seem more hot and romantic. He didn't like it if I called Haze Haze because he said there was a book and a film where a man, not too young, was really after a very underage girl called Lolita, whose surname was Haze. Ilesy seemed to think I was getting at him for being a lech and a perv. Most probably he believed he was more like someone we did in a poem at school – the young Lochinvar, who was dauntless in war and had the best steed in the Borders. He carried away a girl called Ellen on it just when she was getting married to someone else . . . But Iles lays off Haze now. Eventually he saw she had a proper boyfriend called Scott Grant, about her own age, Sometimes I think Hazel is disappointed.'

'Dandruff princess,' Hazel replied.

The four of them went into the big sitting room. This was where Harpur's wife Megan's books used to occupy shelves to the ceiling on three walls, but Harpur had got rid of most of them and the shelves not long after her death. He said, 'I don't want to be inhospitable, Mrs Gaston, but I must be on my way in a few minutes.'

'We could talk to Mrs Gaston, Dad, and tell you later what it's about,' Jill offered at once.

'Well, no,' Harpur said. 'That might not be acceptable to Mrs Gaston. You said, Jill, that Mrs Gaston would like to talk to me personally.'

'We could tell you personally afterwards what she and we said,' Jill replied. 'It would be personally, but personally from Mrs Gaston through Haze and I.'

'Haze and me,' Harpur said.

'No, not you, because you wouldn't be there, would you? That's the point. Haze and I,' Jill said.

'Haze and me,' Harpur said. 'Grammar.'

'What about it?' Jill asked.

'Oh, God,' Hazel said.

'Some matters are not for general discussion,' Harpur said.

'This wouldn't be general.' Jill said. 'Just us.'

'Drop it, Jill,' Hazel said. 'You know what he's like. He won't change.'

Harpur saw that Jill was trying to think of an answer to this, but in the pause Mrs Gaston said, 'I'm housekeeper at Mr Jack Lamb's home, Darien.'

Jill switched. 'Ah, Dad knows Jack Lamb. It's a business matter, a special business matter.'

Perhaps this explained why Harpur thought he recognized Mrs Gaston. He must have seen her at Jack's place during the murder inquiry, or on a previous visit, but hadn't taken particular notice.

'Yes, a business matter,' Jill said. 'Jack's not so bad when you know him, is he? If it's just his voice on the phone, that's different – creepy, and smarmy, like announcers on Classic FM radio. Dad puts it on sometimes when he's wanting a bit of a pick-me-up from Fred Handel.'

'I'm ashamed to say I'm a smoker,' Mrs Gaston replied.

'No need to feel bad about that,' Hazel said. 'It's a free choice. You're entitled. I don't believe people should be forced to give up something they like because the government and others say so.'

'What's known as "the nanny state",' Jill said. 'Like rich people have a nanny to look after their children and order them around. Interfering. The nanny state tells us it's for our own good. Oh, yeah? Dad's girlfriend, Denise, smokes, doesn't she, Dad? Yes, it makes her mouth and clothes rather smelly but Dad puts up with it because he loves her, don't you, Dad? He knows he's lucky. She's much younger than Dad. She's nineteen, only four years older than Haze. But not underage. Dad might object to the smoking, but not enough to put him off. She's going to have what's known as a degree, meaning educated plus, so, like Haze says, Denise is entitled to make a choice.'

'Mr Lamb doesn't like any smoking in the house,' Mrs Gaston said.

'Obviously there are people like that. There's a lot of publicity,' Hazel said.

'Smoke gets into the wallpaper like being sucked up by a lung,' Jill said. 'At school they showed us pictures of a smoker's lung. I don't know whether Denise has seen one of those. They're always getting at us with things at school. Sex. A nurse came to talk to the girls and said, "Don't put yourself at risk for the sake of five minutes' pleasure. Any questions?" Angelina Mount said, "How d'you make it last five minutes?"'

'It's the need, the addiction, that I'm ashamed of,' Mrs Gaston replied. 'So when that need comes I have to go into the yard for a quick break. So furtive and grubby.'

'This is not at all unusual,' Hazel said.

'When the smoking ban first began in Ireland someone who'd been away for a while returned and saw women smoking outside a pub. He thought they must be tarts,' Jill said.

'I try hard to get rid of the butts and so on,' Mrs Gaston said.

'Known as PC,' Jill replied. 'Politically correct. This means the people who think they got a right to tell us all how to live would say, "Although it can't be OK to smoke, if a person *does* smoke, regardless, it can be only decent for that person to get rid of the dibbie-ends." Usually, if something is correct, such as the answer to a question in an exam, this is excellent. But "politically correct" is goody-goody and obeying dull rules.'

'Anyway, while I was clearing up like this a week or so ago a van appeared on the drive and parked near the house, A man got out, opened the vehicle's rear doors and produced a big suitcase from inside, a suitcase on wheels. He went into the porch to the front door.'

'Ah,' Harpur said.

Hazel said, 'Don't take this badly, Mrs Gaston, will you, but I'm looking at Dad's face? I think I'm quite good at reading what he's thinking, and I get the notion that he already knows what you're saying.'

'He can be like that, Mrs Gaston,' Jill explained gently. 'He knows many varieties and aspects of things, but he doesn't mention them. All police are like that, most probably, but Dad especially. Do you have the info re this van, already, Dad?' Jill asked.

'Let Mrs Gaston go on,' Harpur said, 'as long as it's brief.'

'Mr Lamb must have opened the front door of Darien himself, and when I went back into the house, I could hear his voice. He was obviously angry.'

'Saying what?' Hazel asked.

'To do with pictures. There was that awful trouble at Darien, as you know, and it seemed to be mixed up with that, and also about money,' Mrs Gaston said.

'What money?' Jill asked.

'Mr Lamb was saying some pictures were worth a lot more than that money,' Mrs Gaston said.

'But which money?' Hazel said.

'I didn't hear which,' Mrs Gaston replied.

'What was in the suitcase?' Jill asked.

'Don't know,' Mrs Gaston said. 'I can't say if the suitcase was even opened. I could hear the two of them, but not see. They might have been just into one of the downstairs side rooms with the door open. It wasn't friendly talk.'

'So what did the other one, not Jack Lamb, say?' Hazel asked.

'Sorry about his mother being jailed only for trying to protect the gallery and Jack himself,' Mrs Gaston said. 'A disgrace. And therefore some people wanted to help Jack, which was the reason for the visit. But Jack said he didn't want their help – he said their effing help, but I'm thinking of the children, Mr Harpur – and it wasn't help anyway, it was trying to cash in on a disaster. So get effing lost.'

'And he did, did he?' Hazel asked.

'That was the end?' Harpur said.

'You knew it all already, did you, Dad?' Hazel said.

'Not quite the end,' Mrs Gaston said. 'I was driving down to the town for some shopping not long afterwards and in a layby a few miles from Darien I saw three vehicles. I wouldn't have thought much of that but one of them was the blue van. An Audi was parked behind it, very close, and there was another car, maybe a Ford, a little way away, and a man and a woman standing near it, talking.'

'Blue van man?' Jill asked.

'I don't think so. I didn't get a really good look at any of it because I needed to keep driving. I had to decide which reg number to remember because I couldn't do all three as I passed. I hadn't fixed on the van number when it was at Darien because I thought there was nothing unusual about it – just delivering ordered goods. It was only when I heard Mr Lamb shouting that I realized the situation wasn't normal. So I've got the van's number, but not the other two's. We've all been tense at Darien because of the shooting, which is why I thought I should talk to you, Mr Harpur.'

'So right, Mrs Gaston,' Jill said.

Mrs Gaston took a piece of paper from her bag and gave it to Harpur. 'The van reg,' she said.

'Thank you,' Harpur said.

'Dad has to go, but I'll make us some tea,' Hazel said.

'There are scones,' Jill said.

TWENTY-THREE

Harpur heard from behind him the door to the chapel open and then a few quick, discreet footsteps. He assumed it must be a latecomer to the funeral and didn't look around. He thought that would have seemed nosy and disapproving. But Iles, in the pulpit, facing towards the congregation, and about to begin with whatever in his special style he'd chosen to begin with, paused for several moments and gave a small, sympathetic smile as if to welcome the new arrival while he or she found a seat. Observing him, anyone who had never come across Iles before would decide that here was kindness, tolerance and general good nature in a top-of-the-range, brilliantly cut ceremonial uniform.

And, based on present evidence, this would be a reasonable view. But present evidence was limited. His behaviour could be markedly unlike today's – today's so far – depending on . . . well, ultimately depending on the type of building he was in. The architecture and acoustics of big-time, ornate, steepled churches could really get up Iles's nose at funerals. Incense, if there was any, also got up it. Whereas, if the proceedings took place in a more humble and/or workaday setting – say a mission hall or, like Thomas Wells Hart's this morning, at the plain crematorium chapel – his attitude might be in remarkable contrast. The comparative simplicity worked a change on the assistant chief, persuaded him into decent, unfeverish, non-loutish behaviour, so that he became almost stable, and seemed well on the way to quite a spell of conditional sanity. Harpur thought the knuckleduster and cuffs might not be called for. This delighted him. He'd always felt certain that these were not the correct kind of kit for use at a funeral, or even brought ready for *possible* use. He had to be equipped in case, though.

A little while ago Iles had explained his differing attitudes to these rites. 'What I need is pricks to kick against, Col,' he'd explained.

'You've known plenty of those, sir.'

'What?'

'Pricks.'

'In a different sense, Col.'

'Which is that?'

'You'll remember from your Sunday School days how God asks Saul, bound for Damascus, to do some ethnic cleansing, why he is persecuting Him; and tells Saul that kicking against the pricks – meaning, in picture language, against an all-powerful Creator – is a no-win mug's game, particularly as, in Middle East style, Saul probably had only sandals on with no socks. The cactus-type pricks could really get at his toes with their jabbing. The modern, non-Middle East version of kicking against the pricks would be running one's head against a brick wall or trying to get the toothpaste back into the tube.'

The pricks Iles wanted to kick against were not easy to define, but Harpur knew the ACC did feel that the 'damned, self-satisfied, burly, grey, exposed stone' of historic churches was present deliberately to taunt and ridicule him by lasting for so many centuries, and being virtually certain to last for many more. This made him feel temporary and fleeting and merely like other people: i.e., short-term. Pointedly, he'd asked Harpur once what the hell he, Iles, had been created for, with his questing mind, exemplary legs and strongly demarcated eyebrows, if he wasn't given the necessary time.

'Time for what, sir?' Harpur had asked.

'Yes, exactly, Col, time.'

Harpur guessed the ACC meant time to get a decent proportion of people globally, women as well as men, to observe these Ilesian qualities – plus several more – and react with instant glad wonderment. Wasn't this daft curtailment of his life wasteful, profligate?

'What d'you think of effigies?' Harpur had replied.

'These are attempts to humanize some of that smug, sacerdotal stone,' Iles had said. 'Or, reversing the process, to turn some of that humanity into perpetual, adamantine stone. Farcical, pathetic, doomed, yet I sympathize.'

'Effigies can show eyebrows pretty well,' Harpur said.

'I wouldn't object if you suggested a job of this kind be done on me in due course, Col.'

'Clearly, not before then, sir,' Harpur had promised.

'When?'

'The due course. I'll write a reminder card for the office so I can regularly check whether the due course has arrived.'

At today's service, Iles was now ready to begin his commentary. The small disturbance at the rear while someone took his/her place seemed to be over. Harpur had the notion it would be a woman because along with Iles's look of genial, top-rate patience from the pulpit, Harpur also detected in his eyes, under those exceptional brows, a lingering and purposeful tit, bum, and possibly face inventorying of her. But Harpur still did not turn his head for a gaze.

'Friends,' Iles said, 'I approve so heartily the present practice of calling a funeral not a funeral but the celebration of a life. Hail to thee blithe positive! True, some regard this as evasive and unreal. Well, who considers the real was all that lovely? Not I. Too much of it around in my opinion. Who was it said, "humankind can't bear very much reality?" Mao? Winnie the Pooh? Bob Hope? Why should we let reality advertise itself? Others ask, if it's such an occasion for celebration why don't people speed up death by not looking both ways before they cross the road? But this is shallow, mere playing on words. I believe the celebratory note is especially appropriate for Thomas Wells Hart. Regrettably, I never met him, not while he was clearly alive, but I know him to have been a splendid and gifted professional. He was, I'm sure, brilliant in his vocation.'

Harpur relaxed. There would be no Desilesian vaudeville today. None of the special irritants designed to set him off was present, although a marvellous collection of these existed. And, because he felt untroubled, comfortable, in the crematorium chapel now, Harpur could safely let his mind sneak away to consider at least one other of the ACC's blistering hatreds. For instance, Iles's loathing for bare stone in full-blown churchy churches tied in neatly with another of his religion based bugbears. Iles had once or twice told Harpur he detested the flagrant echo effect often produced by church organ riffs. 'Why the hell should they have a double life?' he'd asked. He said such music 'blared in naves and apses and transepts and those kinds of admittedly sacred sodding spots.' The din bounced off the 'ugly, smirking wall slabs,' and so flourished at least twice, original and copy or copies. 'What we get, Col, is fucking flamboyant fortissimos, chasing one another around the holy, spired, cavernous shack's big innards.' Whereas he – he, Desmond Iles, Assistant Chief (Ops) – he would get only the one go at existence here below, despite his obvious distinction, poise and gorgeous, purgative rages.

The assistant chief's vivid resentment took in not just the echo and the church as a malignant structure but the ancient masons who had trimmed the stone to manufacture that structure and be complicit in the flatulent, multi-impact, boom-boom hymnal. He obviously felt compelled to resist, to counter-attack, when in such places. He did this by occasionally turning vastly stroppy and anti-liturgical at a church or cathedral funeral service; yes, kicking hard at times against the pricks, including Harpur – very much including Harpur – who tried to fight their way up the steps to flush him out of a pulpit.

But funeral services away from these dire, dwarfing places hardly ever set Iles off on one of his jungle-law protest capers. Background recorded organ tunes accompanied the singing today, but it was muted, without off-the-wall repeats. In any case, a man in conventional clothes, no dog collar, but who seemed to be running things, had actually forestalled Iles – either by shrewdness or sheer luck – and invited him to 'address this gathering of relatives and friends of Tom with some commemorative words.' *Invited him!* That is, he actually suggested Iles should take over for a spell. It was surrender before the possible fight had even begun.

This had badly wrong-footed the ACC. He needed resistance. He needed pomp so he could rapidly and rabidly de-pomp it. He had to have pricks to kick against and as the Hart proceedings none showed – the opposite, in fact: these were people who treated him with mysterious fondness and who obviously longed to bask in his forthcoming tasteful address. The room was fairly anonymous and functional, only an ante-area to the ovens, but it did supply a pulpit. Iles would not have to elbow, punch and knee his way into it, though, or battle to hold it. This pulpit stood empty, gagging for penetration. It lacked only a banner with fluorescent lettering, 'Cometh the hour, cometh the assistant chief (Ops.).' The man in charge had smiled at Iles and made a small gesture with his right hand to confirm the invitation. It was as if he knew Iles, and this handover of the meeting for a while had been planned to make his exuberant, crash-ball tendencies unnecessary. Iles, in light-blue, full-dress gear and carrying his cap, nodded acceptance – a single, brief, shockingly polite movement – and had gone forward to take his place there.

Harpur often thought that ordinary language didn't do when the topic was Iles-centred, and many topics *were* Iles-centred: he generated topics. That phrase, for instance – 'took his place in the pulpit' – was factually correct, but it couldn't give any suggestion of the way once into a pulpit the ACC looked exactly right for a pulpit: they seemed sort of part of each other, like a turtle with its immemorial shell, although the ACC was not in priestly robes. Iles had put his silver-trimmed cap aside using a careful, two-handed grip, as if asking a pawnbroker how much he'd lend on it, and make it quick.

He was well into his performance now. All continued serene. 'I have mentioned Tom's vocation,' he said. 'Of course, his vocation borders on another, my own: the police service. He was a detective (private) and I am with you today in the company of a detective (police.) This is Detective Chief Superintendent Colin Harpur, in the third row, with the knife-and-fork haircut. I wouldn't call him renowned exactly but he does get about quite a bit, and he's certainly not entirely without integrity. Yes, true, he was clandestinely banging my wife for a while although I never touched his underage daughter, except the flesh of our hands – palm to knuckles – her palm and my knuckles, or reversed – these might have been in momentary – or not so long as momentary – inadvertent contact when she was serving me tea and a slice of seedy cake in Harpur's sitting room, while he and her sister were also present.

'I say again, while he and her sister were also present, *and* able to monitor everything that took place during those innocent, exclusively cake moments. I'd swear to this on my mother's grave, if she were dead. Life has its snags as well as its boons and we have to take both aboard.' Iles paused, as he often did after mouthing some creaking platitude. It was as if he couldn't now believe he had said what he'd said and needed time to put distance between it and himself and recuperate from the corniness.

These few moments of silence were an invitation. From somewhere behind Harpur, a woman spoke, her voice low but audible, her tone sad, pained and regretful. Harpur recognized it, of course: Judith Vasonne's, last heard at Cairn Close after the shooting. 'Shall I tell you why I am here?' she asked Iles.

Iles dredged up a quick response that could easily have been taken for genuine tenderness and consideration. This was another of Iles's showpieces that Harpur had seen several times in the past. Even so, he still felt startled when it happened. Now, the assistant chief said comfortingly, 'I believe you are here, as are the rest of us, Judith, to mourn, but also, as has been mentioned, to celebrate a life. Positivism is present.' Harpur saw no rage froth on the ACC's lips despite this uncalled for interruption of his address.

'I might have helped put an end to that life,' she said.

'In which respect?' Iles replied, leaning forward over the edge of the pulpit, perhaps to improve contact with her, or get a better position for spitting.

'Death,' she said.

'There *is* a death, certainly, and wreaths,' Iles said.

'And then to have cut him off. Cruel,' she said.

'To cut off his life?' Iles asked.

'My mobile. To deliberately disable it. He would have no one to call for support,' she replied. 'I know I didn't mention this when we were all at the close. I felt too much guilt.'

'Which kind of support?'

'This is how I try to compensate,' she replied.

'By coming to the funeral?' Iles said. 'He would appreciate this, I'm certain. From what I've heard, I believe he was that kind of person – appreciative, and especially appreciative of someone making it to his funeral, despite possible delays en route, perhaps leading to entirely excusable lateness.'

'Maybe. He'd grown a little distant, a trifle indifferent,' she said. 'That's what the years can do. No good complaining.'

Iles came effortlessly back to full, rosy Ilesness. 'Yes, yes complain. Fight it. Do not go gentle. Let time know how you abhor it. Who was it referred to "sluttish time" – Bismark? Joe Louis? Ché?'

To address her, Harpur did turn now. 'Mr Iles has a long-standing grievance against time,' Harpur said, '–that he's unlikely to get enough of it. Although this grievance is longstanding by normal standards it is not as longstanding and will not be as longstanding in the future as the stone walls of cathedrals.'

'Time? In fact, our best, most brilliant, time was when I ludicrously proposed a career in feet for him and then, almost immediately, exposed and condemned this as a *lumpen* waste of his flagrant potential,' she replied. 'Feet are not negligible, but nor were they right for Tom. I should have seen that sooner. Reject! Reject! Reject!'

Iles said, 'In his forgivably plonking style Harpur will probably point out that being, as Tom was, a gumshoe is not all that different from a career in feet, since feet have to be placed in those gumshoes if the gumshoe is to do a gumshoe's work.'

Harpur said, 'Being, as Tom was, a gumshoe is not all that different from a career in feet, since feet have to be placed in those gumshoes if they are to do a gumshoe's work.'

'True, Col,' Iles said.

'If necessary I could have convinced him that there were plenty of other people, including some from the school we were both at then, who would give proper care to the community's feet,' she replied. 'He need not feel guilty of abandoning this occupation before he had even started it.'

Most of the congregation were looking towards Judith, now. Some of them, and possibly most, would only have attended the funeral because they'd heard Iles was due there and liable to go into one of his entertaining famed fits of prime obsequies ructions. They might not even have heard of Thomas Wells Hart, but Iles had become part of the city's folklore, and information about him and his intentions circulated continuously, especially in the matter of funerals. This wouldn't be exactly the sort of carry-on they were expecting, but a fair substitute.

Judith was standing in the aisle. Harpur found he had her very accurately in his memory: she'd be about twenty-seven or -eight, tall, slim but busty, oval faced, natural fair to blonde hair worn to just below her ears, blue eyed, strong, short nose, wide mouth that could probably offer a good grin, but didn't now. She had on a long, navy-belted great coat buttoned up to her throat and a black, trilby style hat. The coat fitted close and emphasized her slimness. 'But perhaps I shouldn't interrupt,' she said suddenly and sat down on a nearby chair.

The ACC quivered. All that was visible of his upper body above the rim of the pulpit had a thirty-second, very thorough tremor. In his right cheek this tremor promoted itself into an occasional serious twitch. The distinguished insignia on his shoulders bunched up like a drunk tailor's work, then settled flat and authoritative again. Harpur knew that this kind of abrupt, knees-bent, drop to a chair or bench or settee by an attractive, young woman could deeply stir Iles, not so much spiritually as otherwise. He'd mentioned to Harpur that he could visualize in exact, useful detail the way her body made frank contact with the surface of a seat, although it was through a couple of layers of clothes, one of them possibly silk and in a promising pastel shade, far be it from him to mind which. His voice weakened for a moment once more, became hoarse and faint, and then recovered. 'Please do not criticize yourself. Good interchange with those assembled to pay respects is always welcome,' he fluted.

'Perhaps we could talk better at the post occasion piss up,' she replied.

'That would be grand,' Iles said.

'No! No! Whatever has to be done and said should be done and said here while he is still with us.'

Harpur, like Iles, had been watching Judith take her seat, Iles still with the shakes. She hadn't spoken after her suggestion of a later meeting. The voice that shouted those words, was a woman's, but a different woman's; a very powerful voice, and despite the plainness of the setting it managed to get quite a decent echo. The actual spoken double 'No' came over as four or even six. Harpur's gaze switched to her. This woman was sitting at the end of a row on the far right of the chapel. She'd be late forties, Harpur thought, probably mid-height, rugged, aquiline face, plentiful grey hair. She stayed seated. Like Harpur, most of the congregation adjusted their field of view so as to examine this new heckler.

She said, 'Do we really need such language?'

'Do who need it?' Iles replied.

'All who are assembled here,' she said. 'Do not they – we – deserve more respect than this?'

'Which language?' Iles asked.

'"Piss up". Isn't there a less crude term available, given the nature of this gathering today? Judith Vasonne wants to sound worldly, uncowed by the circumstances. Typical. Egomaniac. Devious. Ingratiating.' Harpur reckoned that the period gaps between these snarled words were of exactly equal lengths as though they had been prepared and rehearsed ready. She couldn't have known the term 'piss up' would be available as a prompt, but she'd probably have found some other way of sourcing her string of slurs. Who was she? And why did such hate for Judith flow from her. He wondered whether Iles, with his famous intuition could work it out. But, in any case, answers began to show themselves now.

'You put him into that box, Judith,' the older woman declared, 'and what has to be said should be said while he and the box are present. This is the culmination of a narrative. It demands a fullness, agonizing and tragic though this fullness might be.'

'Oh, hell, it's you,' Judith said.

'Your disgraceful appetite,' the other said, and Harpur began to realize who she must be. Iles had probably got to it minutes ago.

He had emerged totally from his spasm, still bent forward over the edge of the pulpit and smiling cheerily said, 'This is liveliness. This is ding and dong. And a name. We have a name? Here is Judith, as we know. He nodded in her direction. And?' he said, turning towards the older woman.

So, no, Iles's near-magical insights hadn't unlocked these mysteries yet. Or, he wouldn't admit they had. He knew only the same as Harpur. Or did he?

'She's Daphne, and a malevolent, obsessive, big-words cow,' Judith said. 'Narrative!'

Iles said, 'Taught with you? Disapproved of you?'

'I sought decency,' Daphne said. 'I sought rectitude, nothing more than normal, basic rectitude. And she, Judith Vasonne, as she was then, and Thomas Wells Hart, perverted this wish by contemptuously resisting my mission. Thomas Wells Hart turned it into profit for himself.'

'She put a snoop on Tom and Tom made a monkey of him. Pinched his job,' Judith said.

'And so look at how he is now,' Daphne replied. 'Pinched the job and so landed the chance to die young. I have kept track of you, Judith. You went away, yes, married, I understand, but then someone tells me you've been seen here at The Knoll – seen with *him*. Such effrontery still! I could not let you carry on in life as if you had done no blundering wrong. This occasion would have been incomplete if I had not determined to speak all I knew. What you have heard from me this morning will give you an extra topic to discuss at your disgusting, unfeeling "piss up",won't it?' She stood, glanced towards the coffin, bowed slightly, then walked slowly down the aisle and out into the street. It was a steady, meaningful walk with a bit of a thump to it, and Harpur thought she wanted to proclaim finality: all that needed to be spoken had been spoken and in suitable circumstances. End. She was wrong, of course, but for the moment Harpur didn't know how to put her right.

'There we are then,' Judith said, 'she's given us her bilious piece. I think you should perhaps get on with your commentary, Mr Iles. Sorry about the bitch interloper. She hasn't changed, except to get uglier and louder and primmer. Please resume. You had mentioned your sidekick, Harpur.'

'Yes, Harpur,' Iles replied. 'It is Harpur who will be hunting down whoever killed Tom Wells Hart, on my . . . on *our* ground. Col probably possesses already many secret factors about the case that he hasn't disclosed to me. He tends *not* to disclose matters to me, especially if they're important. A kind of immaculate sliding-scale prevails: the more crucial the information he has, the more one would expect Harpur to consult me about it, and the less likely he is to do so. Think about this, would you, please? I am the assistant chief constable, brackets, Operations. That is my official, recognized designation. The brackets might seem to make this word unimportant, a bit added on – the way they put some lords' first names. No. It defines an area of responsibility, a vital area of responsibility.

'Now, what Harpur is engaged on is unquestionably an operation. What else could it be? Therefore, or *ergo* as Latinists might say, you'd assume he would report his major operational findings

to me, his line manager. I fear you don't know Harpur. I get a
load of *premier cru* silence. It's his housewifely practice, adding
in private to his cosy little store-cupboard. I had the impression
when meeting him today, for instance, that he'd just come upon
something very useful. Yes, this very a.m. Possibly a caller turned
up at that property of his with unexpected goodies. He lives in
an extremely ripe-for-renewal district of the city. With no regard
for social quality and rating, he stubbornly persists in bringing
up his daughters there, including the lovely one I've categorically
never laid a hand on, other than palm to knuckles, or knuckles
to palm.' Using his own two hands he gave a demonstration of
how these meaningless, unerotic, even *anti*-erotic, mini-collisions
might have occurred during a tea and seedy cake occasion. He
said, 'Harpur was slightly breathless and jumpy, as if he had just
received a considerable surprise, probably a good, considerable
surprise.

'Yes, my information is cruelly Col-redacted, but I understand
that, because Tom was going on a dangerous assignment, he had
cleared his pockets of all items that might offer insights to an
enemy. In other words he was willing for the sake of his work
to become a non-person, a *sans papiers* – a no-i.d. – as some
are labelled in France. But his actual character and spirit were
so vigorous that they would survive this temporary partial blot-
out of himself. He could be identified easily from his car registration, it's true, but what I mean is his determination not to
provide any search of his clothes with indications of his present
investigations. He made himself a nobody, yet he was always a
much admired, much loved, *somebody*, as this turnout here today
proves so well.

'Harpur, despite certain unamusing, chronic character weak-
nesses, will bring his killer, his killers, to trial and demonstrate
worldwide that Thomas Wells Hart's death deserves and will
receive investigation by the best officer available: Col.'

People at a funeral do not applaud but there was a grateful,
widespread, warm murmur of thanks, even though some would
have noticed the ACC's shudder episode and feel cheated that it
hadn't progressed into something authentically rough-house and
crazed. When Iles came back to his seat. Harpur, alongside him,
said, '. . .'

But why Harpur again?

Why? Prats! Can't you see? It's because Iles still needed something to kick against after so much conversation and not much else.

Harpur said, 'You graced this congregation with a resounding, much appreciated tribute to someone whose garments you so deftly yet sensitively rifled right there at the death scene, sir, no shilly-shallying, no fear of blood, no abject serfdom to protocol and dogmatic police procedural rules. Pro-active would be my term for this – pro-active in its most pro-active form. Your steady handling of the interruptions was notable and positive. You drew these revelations from them as no one else could have. Your remarks about Hart's empty pockets brilliantly left out the fact that you yourself had done the search.'

'Thanks, Col,' Iles replied. 'I treasure your approval, of course, in my fashion.'

'Which fashion is that, sir?'

'Mine.'

'Anyway, my deepest and most sincere congratulations, sir.'

Heart-to-heart, Iles replied, 'Just don't fuck up, you jerk, now there's some extra material, that's all.'

TWENTY-FOUR

S o, I'd watched the recent mysterious playlet at Jack Lamb's place, Darien, and then taken an ad-lib speaking-part in the layby presentation a little later. Upshot? Obvious: I had to backtrack hard and recognize that I'd probably been stupidly wrong at The Knoll to dismiss Judith's worry about her brother as alarmist flim-flam. I'd just landed the partnership at that time and felt cocky enough to believe absolutely in my instinctive and instant ability to read a situation accurately. I'd lacked caution. I'd learned some since. I was learning more now.

OK, I admit I didn't have an identification for blue-van-man, and couldn't be sure he must be Keith Vasonne. Nor did I know for certain – really *know*, not just guess at – what the wheely contained, and how it figured in the encounter with Lamb, if it did.

But Judy had said she suspected her brother might be into dodgy art dealing at Darien, after Lamb's mother's shoot-out. I'd viewed what might be something like that, hadn't I? Coincidence? Could be.

I was bound to wonder, though, whether what I'd witnessed today made Judy's anxiety seem justified and sensible; not only witnessed: I'd joined in. Shouldn't I have realized that Judy wasn't the kind to panic and fantasize possible big danger for her brother? We'd been close enough a few years ago for me to understand how her mind worked. Most likely this wouldn't have changed. She'd have her reasons for what she'd said, and strong reasons. Because she'd been a Religious Education teacher years ago, it didn't follow that she had a taste for hocus-pocus.

I *did* realize, of course, that it was no crime to look for bargains at a gallery hit by rough and very grave trouble: say, the owner's holidaying elderly mother jailed for gunfire manslaughter on the premises, almost murder. To keep the business alive and the cash flow flowing it might have to drop prices for quick sales. Any commercial outfit in trouble did this. Likewise the stock exchange.

Buyers would naturally, and legally, swoop to take advantage. After all, why else were the reductions offered?

But . . . oh, yes, there's a but: but, for art trading, a core question might have to be faced, and faced first: is the customer's, or customers', intended purchase money clean? *How come you got so rich in the readies, mate? You want to take us into something unwholesome?*

Pics, and to a lesser extent sculpts, had become a very preferred method of investing, and nicely laundering, crooked cash: drugs sales cash; blackmail pay-offs; extortion income; kidnap ransoms; protection fees; and more protection fees; fraud profits; robbery hauls. This is money that cannot be held in a bank or building society or in stocks and shares because it would be conspicuous and liable to bring dangerous attention from the Treasury and the police. Major villains, loaded with splendid but awkward, deeply incriminating, bales of raw, unlawfully piled up currency, might not know much about art but they did know what they liked: safe and extremely respectable 'placement', to use a trade term; placement for hot, hazardous sterling or dollars or euros; these placements – actually *re*placements – likely to appreciate at a jolly speed, especially as they were bought knockdown cheap: low start, fast rise; 'Lazarus leaps', as the process was known, after the New Testament celebrity who came back from the dead.

The works acquired in this type of slippery, confidential deal would probably never get displayed in some gangster's drawing room for his/her spouse or aunty or neighbours or accomplices to enthuse over; to envy and guess at a six- or seven-digit value already, and growing; the entire process more or less pure: well, in fact, more less than more. The trouble with admirers was that they might rapturously and carelessly talk elsewhere about these beautiful items, their fortunate new proprietor and the address they gloriously bedecked. Eventually well-documented whispers would possibly reach the Metropolitan Police's anti- Proceeds Of Corruption Unit (POCU), and/or one of the law's fine-arts detective squads here, or in the United States or Japan or Dubai or China, or almost anywhere in Europe. 'Global': this was the reputation of great pictures, their charm, their impact, international. Obviously, such reputations wouldn't have flowered unless the works had been on public view at some happy time in the past. However, very unwise now.

Art critics sometimes praised a picture for being subtly understated, though not anything by Jason Pollock or Frank Auerbach. But works that became elegant parts of the laundering process didn't state anything at all, subtle or otherwise; not to outsiders, anyway. They were craftily kept concealed, until re-sale. In fact, they might be not simply under*stated* but sequestered under*ground,* in a temperature-controlled, dust-free, utterly private strongroom – concrete walls and roof, reinforced steel door, multi-locked – built for this purpose in the owner's cellars, and looked in on now and then or oftener exclusively by him/her.

These visits would not be simply or even mainly for quiet, contemplative aesthetic pleasure – say, delight in perspective, light and shadow, eloquent portraiture, colour range and accuracy – but to check that no sly and greedy bastard had got into the property somehow, forced the locks and nicked the whole fucking classy lot, total *dis*placement, like that famous swiping raid on a gallery in Boston USA. Once works from a private strongroom had been stolen they would most likely stay stolen. Their owner could not report this loss to the police because there'd be intrusive and very focussed inquires about how the owner came in fact to *be* the owner. The answer was clear: plunder. That's what they'd been bought with. The owner wouldn't want to give this answer, though, nor even to be asked the question.

To keep a deterrent Rottweiler in the strongroom would be risky. The beast might get heavyweight playful and take bites out of the pictures and/or pulverize exquisite figurines. Pity the collector. Enjoying triumphant thoughts of future auctions he/she might open the metal door one morning and find the guardian dog with fragments of a blue, glowing, waterlilies job by Monet in the dangling, rhythmically swaying strands of its muzzle drool.

OK, the owner might have a gun in the house somewhere and, in an absolutely understandable, culture-based fury, get it and shoot the sodding vandal: a due, wholehearted rejoinder on behalf of art, loveliness and the soaring Beijing market. This could make further mess, though, plus the difficulty of removing the corpse. A shot Rottweiler could produce quite a lot of blood and bone fragments.

I thought Judy's worries about Keith came in two kinds. First, she might be scared on her own and their parents' account that he'd get drawn into crime and possible arrest and humiliating conviction for handling loot. Incidentally, perhaps Jack Lamb felt similarly nervous about possible disastrous tangles with the law. I wondered if at Darien I'd watched Keith Vasonne arrive with a case full of funds, wanting to make an offer for some of Lamb's treasures. I didn't think the money would be Vasonne's own. Judy hadn't hinted at that. He might be acting as a go-between courier for someone else: someone of grander crookedness and vaster opulence who didn't want to risk a personal appearance, and/or who regarded haggling as beneath him/her now. This would suggest that Keith, if it *was* Keith, must be well trusted and, therefore, not a novice in the laundering vocation.

It looked as though Lamb had refused to deal. Although he might need trade and income he quite possibly didn't fancy Vasonne's kind of trading, suppose it *was* Vasonne. Lamb would already be finding life tense. There'd been the shooting, the sending down of his mother, plus the disturbing fact that, because of the killing in his home and gallery, police would have swarmed all over the property, undoubtedly giving attention to the art work he had there, and wondering about where it had come from – its provenance, to call on another piece of trade jargon – and its genuineness, or not. No matter how keenly Lamb needed to make some sales, he would know he had to keep clear of anything suspect, at least for a while. Perhaps he even feared blue-van-man could be an attempted stitch-up by the police.

The second, and much worse, cause of Judith's dreads was that she might fear for Keith's physical safety, perhaps for his life. Because art deals often involved very big money, they could also involve very hard and ruthless people. She possibly doubted his ability to cope in that dicey game. Profits from illegal art trading now ranked third in criminal earnings, only drugs and armament more. This meant competition, sometimes brutal competition, and sometimes lethal. I, Thomas Wells Hart, can vouch for this, of course, if I'm allowed to comment, admittedly out of time-order here.

I had Judith's current mobile phone number and decided I might sometime fairly soon give her a ring. I'd intend it as an admission of regret for not immediately seeing at The Knoll that her concern might signal genuine crisis. She hadn't actually grown visibly enraged by my attitude then, but I'd sensed her disappointment, even, possibly, a sliver of contempt – 'Chicken!' – though she wouldn't say it. 'Betrayal!' – though she wouldn't say it: betrayal of that risk-taking happiness we'd had when I was younger and less timid. I still didn't fancy trying to bug the conference room at her brother's house, but I'd be willing to talk about other ways to discover what was going on. Other *positive* ways. That in itself would demonstrate how ashamed and sorry I felt for my previous indifference. No need to make an apology: it would be built-in. The change of approach should tell her that I wanted to make up for the time we might have lost through my blindness. I felt I'd come over as someone acquainted with humility now and no longer a brassy, knowall twerp. I'd give her a description of blue-van-man and she should be able to say whether he might in fact be her brother. I thought he almost certainly was. And I thought, too, that he was probably much deeper into crookedness than she feared.

TWENTY-FIVE

From BW to all staff,

Please note that the attached contract with Ms Daphne Davenpole is for a period in the first instance of one week only. Ms Davenpole requests covert surveillance of Miss Judith Vasonne, a teacher colleague, and Thomas Wells Hart, a pupil at the school where the two women work. Ms Davenpole did not say why she wanted surveillance carried out, but I have agreed that the firm will provide the specified service for seven days, at the end of which either side may close the arrangement without penalty or explanation. It should be regarded as a trial exercise and subject to revision and/or cancellation. It is obviously possible that Ms Davenpole's motive in booking the surveillance contains emotional/sexual elements. Embarrassment might have prevented her from speaking of this to me. Naturally, she is entitled to her silence, but the agency needs to act with exceptional sensitivity and discretion in these circumstances, especially as to-date no apparent criminal offence is involved. All parties are adult.

Narrative reports of the surveillance results together with any relevant photographs will be submitted daily to the agency and sent on to Ms Daphne Davenpole immediately either by courier or e-mail. For convenience and confidentiality the two parties under surveillance should be referred to only by the initial letter of their respective surnames V and H. Ms Davenpole has supplied the agency with home addresses of V and H, and a school sixth form photograph in which H appears as well as V and some other teachers, though not Ms Davenpole herself. V lives alone in a one-bedroom flat. H lives with his parents and siblings in a semi-detached four-bedroom house. Her thoroughness in providing these items suggests consider-able strength of purpose. We have no certainty of that purpose, though, and this is a further reason for carefulness.

                              Bainbridge Williamson.

Of course, once I was a partner I had the run of all the agency's job records. And – another of course – I'd wanted to examine the one labelled MS DAPHNE DAVENPOLE. It was sure to involve me. Although I wouldn't rate a file of my own marked THOMAS WELLS HART, I was sure to get a mention, mentions, in hers. I was why she'd asked for the surveillance, I and Judith.

The Righton private inquiry office was a large, three-storey, converted, Edwardian house in Marsh Road. Bainbridge Williamson had kept the property's original name: Mafeking. What had once been a main bedroom in the front now housed the agency's 'Archive and Library'. Few of these spacious houses in Marsh Road functioned as family dwellings any longer. Most of Righton's neighbours would be private practice dentists, nursing home patients and medics, other private investigation firms' personnel, beauticians, independent television production companies, accountants, financial advisers. Two walls in Mafeking's Archive and Library had shelving from floor level to the ceiling. Beige cardboard files were arranged alphabetically under clients' names.

Three work stations stood near a window looking out on to Marsh Road. Most of the documents in the cardboard files were computer downloads: Bainbridge didn't trust electronic memories and liked to have paper, hard-copy versions as well as the same material available on screen. I, too, preferred paper and on one quiet afternoon, hunting for a giggle as much as anything else, I took down the Davenpole file and opened it to that contract and attached typed note from Bainbridge, at that time sole head of the firm.

He would become rather prosy and philosophical now and then when discussing the nature of what he called 'the private investigation profession'. An agency like Righton had to be 'morally neutral', he'd told me several times. 'Our loyalty is to the person or persons who hires, hire, us, Tom, not unlike the responsibility of a defence lawyer, or mercenary solider.' Bainbridge would admit that in, say, certain divorce cases it might sometimes be almost impossible to abide by this rule. One party could seem considerably more guilty of the marriage breakdown than the other. But if he or she were Righton's client the agency's duty was to get the best settlement possible for him or her.

'Morally neutral' evidently didn't mean the same as plain 'neutral'. The agency was partisan, was not at all neutral, was wholly committed – wholly committed to the cause of whoever paid to hire it. And whoever paid to hire it might not be all sweetness and light and respectability. No matter. The agency had to be indifferent to its clients' failings, unless they were flagrantly illegal and/or evil. Generally, it made no judgement on clients' character and behaviour.

Bainbridge always preached this doctrine. And he seemed to half believe it half the time. But, anyone reading his caveat note would have detected some distaste and antipathy in the write-up of his first meeting with this client, Daphne Davenpole, and in the brutally short time limit allowed. He hadn't followed moral neutrality when he wrote the memo clipped to the Daphne Davenpole file. He must have felt the kind of inquiry she was after might damage Righton's standing. His call for 'exceptional sensitivity and discretion' seemed to show that he found some aspects of this commission worrying, and smelly. I could understand that. I'd recently read a novel, *Letters From Carthage*, by someone whose name I forget. In it a private investigator has to spy on a couple making love in the back of a car. It is a comic but also sordid scene. Perhaps Bainbridge had read it, too – he read a lot, and not just Henry James – and didn't want his agency involved in the same sort of louche, furtive situations. Come to think of it, the author's surname might have been James but not Henry, nor P.D.

The contract was Righton's usual issue: covert surveillance on the two named targets, Ms Daphne Davenpole and Thomas Wells Hart, at £65 an hour, rising to £80 an hour if duties continued past midnight. Fees to be paid weekly. The surveillance would be concerned mainly, if not totally, with occasions when the two were together, or had recently been together. Alone or in other company they wouldn't merit much attention.

All periods of surveillance would be logged, giving exact duration and place. Should the surveillance be discovered by either or both targets the standard contract stated that 'it would be a matter for discussion between the agency and the client whether it should continue regardless.' I've learned since that this kind of decision is always difficult. Successfully covert surveillance lets a watcher see the target(s) behaving unguardedly, normally. Not so when someone knows he/she is being observed. Their behaviour then is deliberately shaped to reveal nothing important and confidential. It becomes a mask. It becomes a closed curtain. The watcher actually helps create what she/he is watching. What he/she is watching is someone aware that he/she is watching him/her and therefore feeds the watcher stuff that won't tell her/him anything much and is going nowhere. There aren't going to be any new revelations.

Plainly, if one of the two spotted the surveillance she/he would tell the other. We are most probably dealing with an intimate relationship here – very intimate – and information about a troublesome development for both would be shared.

All agency staff were insured against personal injury incurred during the periods subject to this contract, but if the agency decided that such discovery brought the detective into acute physical danger from either or both targets, the contract would be cancelled; all Righton participation in the case cease; and any fee due from the client calculated only up to the last completed hour of the surveillance.

I finished reading the contract and moved on to the first of the surveillance reports.

TWENTY-SIX

Thursday May 7 2015
From: Rory Mitchell
To: Bainbridge Williamson

I drove to Gowter Avenue, the address we've been given
for H and his parents and siblings. I parked at some distance
from the house so as to keep a discreet watch. He came out
of the house at 1840 and began to walk south west. I identified him from the photographs supplied. I left my car and
followed him to the Moderator private apartment block
where V has a second-floor flat. He remained there from
1910 until 2140, when he left and walked home, reaching
there at 2212. The area between the two addresses is busy
and well populated. By merging with other pedestrians I
could effectively maintain covert surveillance. I don't think
I was observed by H. En route to the Moderator his mind
might have been pre-occupied with the evening's prospects,
anyway, and less than vigilant. The visit to the Moderator
was his sole purpose. He made no stops and spoke to nobody
on his way to or from there.

The outer door to the block is opened electronically after
visitors have announced themselves over an intercom. H
appeared very familiar with this security system. I decided
to examine it while he was inside the building. I found a
panel of six call buttons, each probably linked to an apartment, and each under a printed surname. The top right was
labelled Vasonne. I didn't press it! I'm not in favour of
coitus interruptus.
H had dealt swiftly with the entrance procedure. I was across
the street, not close enough to see which button he pressed
nor to hear properly what followed. But I did hear a woman's
voice answering. He replied very briefly, though, again, I
couldn't make out the words. I had the impression that the

visit was expected and the entrance formalities therefore very brief. The door was opened, apparently by a remote signal from the flat, and he went in. The door closed automatically at once after him. I could not follow H into the building and did not see him actually enter one of the apartments, but in my view the likelihood is high and could safely be categorized as 'beyond reasonable doubt'.
Accountable time: I began the watch in Gowter Avenue at 1800 and ended surveillance when he returned there at 2212.
Total: 4 hours and 10 minutes.

This was a clever boy: first class honours, Cambridge, and jokey with it. Although they wouldn't have had lectures on gumshoeing there, they *would* have helped sharpen his mind via smart-arse teachers: 'dons', as they're are called at Oxbridge. I could absolutely confirm six of his guesses – intelligent guesses, *very* intelligent guesses: (a) I didn't know I was being shadowed, not on that first there-and-back trip. (b) My thoughts were mainly on the treats ahead, or reminiscing afterwards. (c) I had used the main door call arrangement several times before and could operate it swiftly, like someone advertising the joys of technocracy. (d) The visit had been pre-arranged by phone earlier that day. (e) We kept the front door call brief so I would not be conspicuous waiting. (f) I *was* visiting Judith, and beyond any doubt at all, let alone reasonable, I went to her apartment door, Number 3, on the second floor and let myself in with the key she'd slipped to me at a confidential moment in school weeks ago.

Friday May 8
From: Rory Mitchell
To: Bainbridge Williamson

This was virtually a re-enactment of yesterday, with a slight difference in timing. I began the watch in Gowter Avenue at 1800 as before and he walked once more to the Moderator. He set out at 1830 taking the same route. He was at the flats from 1900 to 2155 and returned to Gowter Avenue at 2226. Once or twice on his way home I thought he might suspect he had a tail, although I managed reasonable cover from other walking folk as before. He glanced behind him a couple of times, but didn't change pace or direction. It might be of no significance. He could have heard something unrelated to the surveillance or me. I will increase my alertness all the same.

Accountable time: From 1800 to 2226. Total 4 hours 26 minutes.

Yes, still a clever boy. There'd been a moment on my way back home on the Tuesday when I glimpsed mirrored in a shop's big window a man behind me, early to mid twenties, just short of 6 ft. and hefty, wearing dark clothes. Nothing much in this, possibly, but I had a fancy that I might have half consciously noticed someone similar, either earlier on that evening, or even on Monday. The repetition – if it was repetition – forced my mind back to this previous possible encounter. Had it been memorized without my realizing it? Perhaps now it was conscripted back to reinforce this later suspicion. Darclad wasn't immediately on my heels but never more than twenty metres away, though occasionally obscured by other people. Considered separately, neither of these sightings – possible sightings – would have troubled me. There were plenty of tallish, solidly made men in their twenties about, quite a few of them wearing dark gear. Wasn't it panicky to feel troubled because I'd seen a couple of them? And why would anyone want to tail me or have me tailed? There was that dreary, bitter piece at the school, Davenpole, but however malign she might be she wouldn't set a snoop on me, on us, surely. Surely?

Well, no, not surely at all, as we know now. But I'd done reasonably all right to think Davenpole at once, even if I tried to dismiss the idea with that 'Surely?' But it was 'Surely' as a question, one touched by doubt, big doubt.

Saturday May 9
From: Rory Mitchell
To: Bainbridge Williamson.

At just before 1800 I took up my usual position in the Clio at the end of Gowter Avenue, allowing a sight of the

house, but not noticeably near. H didn't appear until 1850.
He had a push bike with him. He set off on in the customary
south-west direction. This gave me difficulties. I couldn't
keep up with him on foot, but it would be very obvious if
I held the car at low speed to stay behind him. I decided
to assume he was making for the Moderator building and
drive there independently of him. I could watch him arrive
and leave. After all, this was what the surveillance needed
to discover: times, dates. I'd record events from the comfort
of my car. I chose a slightly different route. I didn't want
to overtake him in case he recognized the Clio from Gowter
Avenue. I would still get to Moderator before him.

He arrived at 1903 and took the bike with him through
the front door. There were no developments until at 2020,
as the sun went down, I saw a red Honda appear from what
must be a private car park for residents behind the Moderator.
From photographs I recognised V at the wheel. H was beside
her. I started the Clio and got into a tailing position. I
followed them to Cordwains country park and lakes, a well
known, secluded spot for backseat couples and doggers.
This surprised me. They didn't need rural privacy. They had
the flat, and the door security.

She pulled up among the trees and both climbed out of
the Honda. It was dusk. They walked together holding hands
down to the lakeside. I'd parked the Clio a little way from
the Honda and for several minutes I had a terrible rush of
very sombre romantic clichés: jinxed, persecuted lovers,
dark waters, night falling. Had they agreed to finish it all?
Was I too far away to stop them? Perhaps he *had* spotted
me tailing him, yesterday or on Monday, had told her and
they'd agreed a drowning pact. 'In their death they were
not divided,' as that Victorian novel says about characters
caught in a flood, pinching the line from the Bible.

As it turned out my fears were foolish, tripey and alarmist.
They walked for a few hundred yards around the lake, still
hand-holding, probably chatting, seeming entirely relaxed;
then returned to the Honda and she drove them back to the
Moderator.

Perhaps they had become a little ashamed of their relationship's furtiveness until now, bored by it. They wanted normality, maybe, and needed to prove to themselves, at least, that there was more to what they had together than sex. They'd take a walk in the park. V might have started this affair because of its daring and defiance of moral rules. Had she grown out of that cheap brand of excitement? I felt touched by their bravery and search for honesty. Accountable time: From 1800 to 2210. Total 4 hours 10 minutes.

Someone – probably Bainbridge – had remarked under this in green ink, 'Felt? Who the fuck cares what you felt? You're supposed to be writing a report not a novelette. And keep your feeble witticisms to yourself.'

In fact, though, Rory's interpretation of what he'd seen was fairly close to the truth, I'd told Judith that I might have been tailed. This enraged her. 'Dotty fucking Daphne Davenpole,' she said. It made her even more defiant and combative than before. She'd said we must go out in the Honda to a notorious mating ground and do some brilliantly nonchalant, entirely wholesome strolling there, to prove we had no sense of guilt or taint. She became very set on this. I went along, though I wondered if this was a wise plan. It seemed confused. We would be visiting a celebrated sex site to have a little innocent hike, and so demonstrate that there was more to us than all that kind of thing, and we didn't care who knew it. Actually, of course, we did care, and the sex between the two of us was a joyful, sweet, probably main factor.

No further reports or mini-novelettes from Rory Mitchell appeared in the Daphne Davenpole file. I could see the reason for this. The Cordswain trip had taken place on May 9th. Next day, back to pedestrianizing, I'd managed to lose him, using that well-known up-and-down-the-aisles supermarket dodge, as featured in crime and spy plays on TV, and had met Bainbridge for the first time in the car park there. He must have decided that any further covert surveillance was impossible. A no-brainer: I obviously knew about it, and, more importantly, knew how to counter it, and make it look farcical. He'd accused Rory of bungling the operation and more or less offered me a job on the spot. Bainbridge wouldn't be giving that kind of work to Rory any longer. And so, no further reports for the file, although they'd been attractively graced with clever insights. Bainbridge wouldn't know that, though, at the time.

He might also have decided that the three reports he *had* received from Rory and sent on to Ms Davenpole were probably enough for her purpose – whatever her purpose might be. There couldn't be much uncertainty about what sort of relationship V and H had. It wasn't all short, fully dressed interludes by Cordswain lake at twilight.

The latest item in the file was a copy of an invoice sent to Ms Davenpole 'For inquiry services as agreed,' and marked 'Paid' in green ink. It contained three entries:

May 7 2015: Observation episode 4 hours 10 minutes
May 8 2015: 4 hours 26 minutes
May 9 2015: 4 hours 10 minutes
Total: 12 hours 46 minutes at £65 an hour.
Amount due: £829.83, but say £800.

There was no charge for time spent on the dismally messed up surveillance of May 10, although it must have been not less than a couple of hours. Bainbridge wouldn't want to admit by making a charge – even a reduced charge – that the Righton firm could be so quaintly hopeless.

TWENTY-SEVEN

Harpur said . . .

But why more of Harpur saying, saying, saying?

Simple: he's one end of a phone chat that could help bring things together a bit.

So, Harpur said, 'Yes, I'll take the call. Put her through, please.'

A delay. Some unexplained background sounds: perhaps a door being shut, a heavy door, maybe a metal door. Then: 'Harpur? You? I'm ringing from the slammer.'

'Well, Mrs Lamb, yes, you would be.' The slammer had metal doors that could be . . . well, slammed, phone booth included.

'Not would be. Am. I *would* like to be somewhere else. But I *am* here. Grammar. I'm hot on it these days. Some of the other prisoners can't read or write, the dears, so I've been giving them lessons. I see a duty to share what education has given me. They call me Brainstorm.'

'That's good,' Harpur said. 'That's considerate and responsible.' Education hadn't kept her out of the slammer, though.

'"Would" is the subjunctive,' she said.

'I think I've heard of that,' Harpur said. 'There's quite a lot of it around, I believe.'

'The subjunctive expresses what's wished for, whereas "I am here" means I'm suppressed, not subjunctive – locked up. It's how jails are. But you know that: clink is your kith. The girls find it funny to be taught English by someone with an American accent. But I tell them I'm as English as they are, but went to America, re-married there. It didn't last. I stayed in the States but changed my name back to what it was, like my son's, Lamb.'

'Yes, of course,' Harpur said.

'We can pay for what's known as a phone facility every so often. It's absolutely secure. And your office switchboard should be the same, I hope.'

'You talk to Jack?'

'Why I'm ringing you. This is something else the girls find

funny – me using up phone cards calling the cop who had me
sent down. They've heard we knew each other pre the Darien
death and ask had we been shagging as a regular thing, but then
I stopped it and so you turned nasty and fitted me up in revenge.
Mostly, these are lovely people, but their thinking is pretty basic.
It's how some of them regard police. Nasty, they believe is cop
default mode. But flattering for me in a way. I mean the age
difference. You like them very young, don't you? Jack's the same.
I gather there's an undergraduate in your life. Right? Denise, is
it?'

'You were waiting for us in Jack's gallery with the gun and
the corpse,' Harpur replied. 'No need for fitting up, was there?
And no detective work. It's a very unusual case. We don't get
many – or, in fact, any – where a woman shoots another woman
surrounded by pictures, some quite probably genuine. I've never
heard of such a shooting in, say, the Tate, although, clearly, plenty
of pictures hang there.'

'Don't the high-ups object to your sleeping with a student not
long out of school?' Mrs Lamb said.

'Fingerprint testing wasn't required. You acknowledged the
shooting at once,' Harpur replied.

'In the States, that wouldn't be a crime. If someone breaks in
to a property and gets shot for it, hard cheese, to borrow an
Orwell phrase.'

'We went for manslaughter, not murder. Best we could do.'

'I'm not going to say "Thank you".'

'I think Jack accepts it.'

'Maybe. I worry about Jack,' she replied.

'In which respect?'

'Yea, yea, "in which respect?".' She gave that a sing-song
touch of *oh, you're so hoity-toity, Harpur*. 'Jack's just a kid.'

'He's done well for a kid – a manor house, and all that goes
with it.'

'No, not all.'

'What's missing?'

'Safety.'

'Nobody's got that in full.'

'Jack's got less of it than most. I'm not talking about the past.
I think of tomorrow, next week, next month. I phone him on the

card and he's full of jokes and bonhomie and jauntiness because he thinks that's what I want to hear. Same when he visits. The round trip is 110 miles but he acts blissfully content, like he's cast as Filial Duty in a Morality play.'

'Yes, he wouldn't want to depress you.'

'He depresses me,' she said. Her voice had moved out of the earlier light bantering tone to a harsh quack-quacking of up-and-coming attack. 'The bouncier he is the lower I feel. He's a kid. He came wearing a busby one day, for a laugh. The screws here didn't know what to make of it.'

'He likes military uniforms. He might have the complete trooping of the colour gear on next time. Some people get a thrill from dressing oddly. I heard of someone who spent a year costumed as a zebra.'

'Look, Harpur, I don't have to tell you your cop-job, do I?'

'In which respect?'

'"In which respect?" I'll tell you in which fucking respect, Harpur. In respect of the previously mentioned tomorrow, next week, next month. All police know, don't they, that if a place gets hit, like Darien got hit—'

'By the woman intruder?'[6] Harpur said.

'By the woman intruder, with a team behind her, most likely. If a place gets hit like Darien was hit, it moves into a new category.'

'What does?'

'The place.'

'Which category?'

'It has become a place that gets hit. Before, it was just a place. OK, it was a big place with a fancy name out of a poetry book, but it was a big place with a fancy name out of a poetry book that didn't get hit,' she said. 'Now it's a big place with a fancy name out of a poetry book that *does* get hit, and there could be another hit, other hits, tomorrow, next week, next month. It's on lists. It's on lists kept by people who are interested in hits. They'll say to themselves, and they'll listen closely to themselves when saying it to themselves, they'll say that if it's been hit it must have things there – items – yes, the owner

6 See *Blaze Away*

must have items there that are worth organizing a hit for. It's true, that first hit failed. Why? Well, not because there turned out to be nothing worth hitting the place for. No, it failed because the owner's mother, i.e., me, happened to be staying there on holiday. She sniffed the approach of trouble, at which she was remarkably gifted and always has been. I don't like to give my second husband, the American, credit for teaching me much, but one special little trick he had did stick. He never left home with less than $1500 on him in case he needed to buy his life from a mugger. His thinking was, expect shit, prepare to deal with shit. I don't go around with $1500 dollars in my handbag but I do try to foresee disharmony and keep equipped to fight it.

'Therefore, Harpur, early on in her stay at Darien this year the mother, viz., self, thoughtfully acquired a piece. Alice Lamb knows and knew how to use a gun, thanks to living in the United States; and knew and knows what a naughty world the world could show itself to be. Yes, this visiting mother has about her a considerable flavour of the United States where matters such as putting a shot or shots into a housebreaker is merely good citizenship. Well, that mother – and I mean not the US curse word some have developed it into by tacking on another – that mother won't be there with her gun tomorrow or next week or next month because she's locked up for a very convenient spell of years before the possibility of parole. "Alice Where Art Thou?" as the old song asks. Answer, "In jug."

'But I'm big here, a celebrity, you know, Harpur. Homicide is prestige, even though it's only manslaughter, not murder. These girls have been caught for petty stuff, most of them. Awe is what they regard me with, top of the range awe. They sense I'm part of a bigger scene. I get asked over and over for my story. I'm Bonnie and Clyde in one. They want details from the burgled, the burglaree, the burglar being unavailable, so they would know where exactly in the house resistance might come from if they matured and were on a breaking and entering sortie themselves. How did I know there was a break-in? Was it something I saw or something I heard? Did I hide waiting to surprise the intruder? Hide where? How did I get the piece, it not being as simple here as in the States? I found an armourer? How?

What model, the piece? How many rounds in the chamber? So, straight arm when you fired? One hand or two on the butt? Or from the hip? One of them might do a sniper crouch, right hand pointing an imaginary Browning. And then her pal will ask me whether I know the gospel.'

TWENTY-EIGHT

'The gospel?' Harpur said.

'The gospel of hits – what I've just been talking to you about. Do you remember from science at school about the amoeba being able to reproduce itself, no second party. Same with hits,' Alice Lamb said.

'Self-generating?'

'Right. During this mother's trial – mine – not much evidence was given in court because I pleaded guilty. A deal had been hatched by the lawyers: admit manslaughter and avoid a possible life sentence if I fought a murder charge and lost. But the media did a lot of background to the case. There were descriptions of the interior and grounds of the house with pictures, and emphasis on the private gallery Jack has created there. This is glorious information for those in the hit and take business. Might as well put a road sign pointing at Darien with a single word on it, "LOOT".

'Background stuff of such quality is scarce. Because there was a glut of it about Darien, the house took a priority in future plans. I've explained this to Jack, as you'd expect, but he smiles and tells me not to worry, says he knows the scene.'

'And he certainly does.'

'What does it mean, "knows the scene"?' she asked in a scathing, ferociously contemptuous voice announcing ahead of the actual answer that "knows the scene" meant bugger all. 'It's gibberish. It's kiddywink, boasty stuff. Knowing the scene's not the same or even near the same as controlling it. In any case, what scene? Define it. There isn't a scene until something happens and by then it's too late to do much about it. Did he know the scene when somebody breaks into the property and he's tucked up snug and intimate with Helen, his young partner. Result? His mother – I – has to deal with a situation which anyone who was supposed to know the scene would have been on high alert for?'

'I think Jack will be OK,' Harpur replied.

'You hope he'll be OK, so you think it. My mother used to say, "The wish is father to the thought".'

'Mothers do make remarks. It's a right the suffragettes strove for.'

'That's not the way the mind ought to work. It's selfish, crazy optimism.'

'Jack's strong. There's more to him than a busby.'

'We come to the gist.'

'Which gist?'

'Are you going to give him protection?'

'In what respect?'

'"In what respect?" Oh, God, Harpur. Two respects. First, in respect of making sure he stays alive and unmaimed. He needs full-time minders. There should be protection at Darien or with him when he goes out. Listen, Harpur, I've been telling the girls the difference between continuous and continual. Continuous means something that goes on and on without a break. Some cinemas have a "continuous performance", meaning you can go in at any time and pick up the story or newsreel. Continual means something that goes on and on but has stops here and there before resuming. A guy might cock-flash continually on a long-haul air flight but not continuously or it wouldn't be flashing but forget-fulness or naturism. Or ventilation. What Jack should have is continuous protection.'

'We don't do that kind of thing,' Harpur replied.

'Which kind?'

'A continuous watch.'

Bollocks. Harpur knew it and had to hope Alice Lamb didn't. In some crises police *would* offer that kind of twenty-four-hour safeguarding for someone considered valuable and at risk. But unique conditions made this impossible for Jack, although he certainly was valuable and might be at risk. Perversely, his massive value worked against him here. Lamb was the greatest informant Harpur had ever dealt with; perhaps the greatest informant any detective anywhere had ever dealt with. That relationship would immediately disintegrate if it became known to villains – and it *would* become known to villains – that Lamb had a cop or cops looking after him and living very close, either continuously or continually.

The rules said that an informant belonged to the whole police force, not simply to one officer. Naturally, Lamb and Harpur ignored this. Lamb whispered to Harpur and only to Harpur, and what he whispered was almost always brilliantly useful. Harpur prized this exclusiveness. His career was part built on it. Predictably, as a businessman Jack expected and got some return. Not cash. A *quid pro quo,* but not a *quids pro quo.* Instead, Harpur had never looked too closely into Jack's art commerce and the back-stories of fine and pricey works he offered for sale.

Harpur could not let this immaculately and sweetly balanced arrangement be disturbed because Alice Lamb was anxious about her 6' 5" and 260lb kiddywinks. Now and then she hinted that she knew or suspected something about the delicate, reciprocal back-scratching agreement between Harpur and her son. Perhaps she thought this connection would strengthen the case for giving devoted, round-the-clock care to someone so helpful. On the face of it, this seemed reasonable. Only on the face of it. The reverse was true. She didn't seem to understand that such special precautions would permanently wipe out Jack's function as a secret source. Although she was a worldly woman who knew about guns and how to cope with a mugging, she apparently couldn't understand the subtleties of running an informant. It was, though, a special craft, with its own very precise and careful regulations and ways of evading them.

In any case, Harpur felt sure Jack would never allow the kind of constant bodyguard companionship Alice wanted for him. She should surely have known this much about her son. She obviously thought him naïve and stupidly, ignorantly happy. Didn't she realize this might be only a front? Jack wouldn't want to make things worse for her by appearing scared. Jail, plus the knowledge that she had slaughtered someone, ought to be enough pain.

'There's no evidence that Jack is threatened,' Harpur said. 'I couldn't justify the kind of manpower, womanpower, you're talking about.'

'Iles wouldn't allow it? Why is he so damn evil and heartless?'

'Yes, Mr Iles can be both of those, or either, though continually, not continuously. He suffers from recurrent sharp, but not life-threatening, fits of galloping seemliness. He's embarrassed about them afterwards, when he's back to his usual malign self. However, I know that whatever state he was in he would not approve the measures you've spoken about. I'll have patrols take in Darien rather more often than is usual for them, but that's the limit.'

'I wonder if you see this situation in full, Harpur,' she said.

'I hope I do.'

'There we go again – hoping. But it's not really hoping, is it, Harpur? This is the polite, English, cold way of giving the brush off. It means, "Of course I know the situation in full, you fucking impertinent cow. It's my job to know it in full."'

'I wouldn't say that.'

'I know you wouldn't. But that's what you mean. When I say "in full", what am I thinking about?'

'The Darien situation, obviously.'

'But what particular aspect?'

'There will be many aspects,' Harpur replied.

'Take the following aspect, Harpur, would you?'

'That's the subjunctive "would," isn't it?'

'Yea. It means I'm not sure you see what I'm getting at, or ever will. Jack tells me he's had at least one approach from people thinking they can buy items cheap at Darien, because of the undoubted troubles there, troubles knocking the reputation of his dealerships. He's turned it or them down. What does that say to you, Harpur?'

'He's strong, he's proud. He doesn't cave in.'

'Yes, that was the kind of tone he used when he told me. It was part of that "keep Ma cheerful" campaign he's running. But what does it actually signify, Harpur?'

'In which sense?'

'In an obvious, practical, simple sequence sense. If he's refused to sell it means there is an interest in these items and – crucially – that the items are still there, doesn't it? Nobody's bought them and taken them elsewhere. Jack wouldn't let the items go. Darien is as much a target as it ever was, possibly more so. And Jack is part of that target.'

Harpur thought this was probably a very acute summing up of things. Jack had told him about the approach and his rejection of it. And the woman on Jack's staff out for a quiet smoke had seen the blue van and its driver make their visit, apparently unsuccessful visit. She'd actually given him the van registration number. That led nowhere, though. Harpur had done a check and found what he expected to find, that the reg didn't exist.

'We'll give Darien max vigilance,' Harpur said.

'Continual.' This was her nuff said voice, her move along voice. 'OK, so the police can't, won't do it properly. I'll go fee-paying. Is there a private eye firm that could take on the chores?'

'Expensive. Anything between £50 and £100 an hour, nights extra.'

'It's my son. I've brought trouble on him. Not many men have a mother who shoots someone dead on his behalf in the family home at night. I've got to compensate. I was counting on you, Harpur.'

'I appreciate that.'

'What d'you mean that you're grateful I thought well enough of you to call for your aid; or you knew I was counting on you? Whichever, you're not going to help, are you?'

'Words are tricky, aren't they: continual, continuous; appreciate, appreciate. The private eye agency is 'Righton, proprietor Bainbridge Williamson,' Harpur replied. 'They've done some good work with us. Hang on. I'll give you their phone number.'

'That's the limit, too, is it?'

'Got a pencil?'

'I said two respects,' she replied.

'Two respects of what?

'Protection.'

'For Jack?'

'Who else?'

TWENTY-NINE

Alice became quiet for half a minute, and when she spoke again it was in a kind of bustling, secretive lecturette tone now. After a few words of it, Harpur realized she was continuing to use an elementary and not too effective code. It seemed to run against her belief that the calls were absolutely secure. She wanted this one to be more than absolutely. 'We come to the second respect. Clearly, there are these certain items at Darien,' she said.

'Clearly. Many.'

'I'm talking about one sort. A particular, valuable sort of item.'

The coding had become fairly ludicrous but he'd play along. 'Yes,' he replied, 'there are unquestionably items present at Darien beyond the standard household gear such as cushions and dustpans.'

'I'm referring to items of value.'

'Yes, of value.'

'You can see, can you, the difficulties as regards these items, Harpur?'

'Difficulties?'

'I don't think that's overstating it. Difficulties, yes. It's my belief they should be removed pronto, in fact, super pronto.'

'The difficulties?'

'The items. Clearly, if the items are removed the difficulties go with them.'

'That sounds neat.'

'The difficulties are integral to the items. The items might be said to come festooned with difficulties. But as long as we recognize this – do not pretend things are simple and easy – we can nullify their impact. This is that second type of protection I referred to.'

'Understood,' Harpur replied. This wasn't true, but he'd prefer not to wrong-foot her.

'These items have been seen, which is not necessarily good; in fact, probably bad,' she said.

'Don't some items exist *only* to be seen? It's what they're for – to get looked at.' Pictures, for instance, though he didn't say so, still not wanting to wrong-foot her. Get it over. Get it over.

'That could certainly be argued. But the crux is, *how* are they, were they, seen, isn't it?'

'There's something in that.'

'This would be a situation where the items are seen not merely by one person, but by several. It's as if I could hear them calling to each other, "Come and look at this one, will you? And, then again, this."' She mimicked high excitement flecked by notions of big money gain. 'We have to ask ourselves, in what circumstances were they seen?'

'This can certainly affect a viewer's reactions,' Harpur replied. 'It's why they have settees in museum art galleries so people can take a rest and not get ratty with the exhibits through tiredness brought on by culture overload. If you're feeling shagged out it's easy to become enraged by a Picasso canvas showing a woman whose nose is where you'd expect her elbow to be, and a face in general like a fractured snow shovel.' Alice probably wouldn't like this reference to galleries and Picasso. It was more or less hinting that the 'items' in their conversation were pictures. Wouldn't anyone have guessed, that though?

'I, personally, am involved in the answer to my question about circumstances,' Mrs Lamb said. 'The handgun, and self behind this handgun, created a situation, and this situation had results.'

'Well, it would.'

'Not would, did. I'm not the subjunctive.'

'Right.'

'What results, you might ask?' she said.

'What results?' But Harpur could see what results. Of course he could. He'd worried about them himself even before this call from the prison phone cubicle. A woman had been shot dead by another woman in a country manor house with its own picture gallery – a spicy event. This had brought a parade of nosy police to the property, and, as Alice Lamb said, they'd seen many . . . well, many items. Some had been on show, others in Jack's basement strongroom, which he'd been required to open for inspection. Although none of the 999 police party at Darien after the killing had been art experts, they'd probably all heard of the various pictures and sculptures scams.

The force's chief detective, Harpur, had naturally been one of the early stage arrivals to deal with the shooting. Although he had his unique, clandestine chumminess with Jack it obviously couldn't function now. The Darien incident was too grave and too colourful and too blatant for blind-eyeing; even by such an accomplished blind-eyer as Harpur. There hadn't been anything he could do for Lamb or his mother. Details about the Darien items were passed on and up to the specialist art and antiques crime unit in London, and this was what Alice Lamb feared. So did Harpur.

'You see,' she said, 'Jack is threatened from two sides, the lawless and the lawful. The lawless fancy Darien as a famous, probably well-stocked objective, already attempted once, but in a doomed, messy way: ripe for a second try. He tells me he's already had a suspect visitor aiming to buy, but really wanting a good look around at the rest of his stuff. Because of what happened previously, the new people might come armed, even if they've heard one of the sharp-shooters – viz. me – is in jail. Jack, trying to resist, might get damaged or worse. He *would* resist – no doubtfulness in that "would". He's not a coward, just a dozy child.

'From the other side, the lawful team will want to know where those valuable items we've mentioned came from. *How* did they come? What is their history? Is there paperwork, e.g., a receipt or two? Were they, possibly, the subject of a snatch, from a public display or private possession, in which case there'd be a glaring absence of paperwork, e.g. a receipt or two? Have some of them been used in money laundering; or are they intended for future laundering? Jack could be on the end of some very unkindly and dangerous questions.

'Hence, Harpur, my two priorities: (a) continuous bodyguard protection, and talk to him about a flak jacket, please. Tell him you know how to get hold of one that belonged to Field Marshal Goering, a portly Nazi: this should chime with Jack's love of uniforms. (b) Removal of the potentially embarrassing items into safe storage elsewhere until the current exceptional pressures fade. The house would have regained its innocence. I'm told this is what we should aim for. Yes, these days I learn as well as teach. There's quite an amount of trade insights circulating here, you know, in the pokey, Harpur. Not all the girls are petty offenders only. Some have had experience with what they call "the daub dicks" – those national, FBI and Interpol arts investigators.'

Although the term 'items' would still occasionally return, Alice appeared to have pretty well given up the coding. She said, 'The girls explain that this brand of detection moves very slowly. Art, and therefore art crime, extends worldwide and inquiries are often complex and tricky and extremely *sans frontières*. But these snoops are very dogged and skilled and, ultimately, very successful, or the girls who talk about it wouldn't be locked up with me, would they?'

'You're something of a saviour, aren't you, Alice?'

'In which respect, as you might say?'

'You shoot someone to make sure Jack is not hurt. Now you want him 24/7 looked after, and would like items that might be incriminating removed.'

'I'm his mother, that's all, Harpur. Just loyalty.'

He sensed this conversation might get awkward. The nature of relationships was going to feature. Mothers had high thoughts about motherhood and it lasted, even when the child was as unchildlike, in appearance anyway, as Jack. 'I'm the law,' Harpur said, an attempt to head off trouble with an uppity, blunt, now-hear-this pronouncement.

'But Jack's a buddy, isn't he?'

'We get on OK.'

'It's more than that, isn't it? Closer, surely?' Harpur heard desperation. She craved a whole-hearted ally on her son's behalf. 'I've watched the two of you. I don't mean gay. But some sort of semi-holy link. You help each other with your different jobs?'

'When appropriate.'

'I hate that word, so deliberately misty and evasive. Officialese. But, all right, I think what I'm proposing is, in fact, entirely appropriate. I'll ask Jack if he'd mind your taking the items and hiding them somewhere suitable, away from Darien, until the crisis is over. It's not the sort of thing he should do himself – very risky: he's too well known around the area. There might be two or three trips needed. I feel sure Jack would agree – but there's that "would" again, in its customary sense suggesting uncertainty, although I've said "I'm sure!". The items would be divided into, say, two or three loads and not difficult to manage manually. Obviously for security's sake it would be best if you carried out this move on your own. The items could be wrapped in plastic and/or sacking. You would have a wholly free choice on where to store them. Jack would approve that, insist on it, I believe. He would trust your know-how.'

'I haven't got much know-how in this profession. I couldn't tell someone's idea of a good hay wain from a bad one.'

'Don't play fucking thick, or thicker than your are, Harpur, OK? I've got limited time on this card. You're privileged. I don't want any of it wasted. When I talk of "know-how" I obviously don't mean know-how about these particular kinds of items themselves, but know-how about where to squirrel them away, out of sight and range of the indecently, malevolently curious. You understand how the indecently, malevolently curious operate because for most of the time you're one of them.

'There is, of course, one obvious and very tricky question. How do you and, indeed, how does Jack, determine which of the items are genuine and therefore worth concealing and which are frauds, possibly churned out by the hundred in a Yeovil factory? Would it be lunacy to carry these also into hiding. Answer? No, it wouldn't. We have to act urgently and fast. We can't fanny around deciding which to include and which not on grounds of authenticity or the want of it. Take the lot, all in one of the fellest of fell fucking swoops. The sorting can be done later when the tension is less.'

'It's going to look odd, isn't it?'

'What?'

'Jack has a fine show place at his home, but with nothing to display there. Yet there were items present when the police last called. What's happened?'

'There's been a killing *chez lui*, hasn't there, Harpur? You're talking to the killer. It might appear natural for the owner to avoid for the moment risk of another break in. So, he gets rid of all stock, possibly putting about that he's waiting for a while before replenishing: "Available soon," as you occasionally see on a beer pump in pubs when a brew has run out. In any case, Harpur, an empty gallery is better for Jack than one that involves scrutiny and probing and maybe some distressing truths. Jack couldn't be charged with possession of a void gallery and store-room. It wouldn't be just the gallery walls that had nothing to inquire about. Neither would Jack's cellar-strongroom. All stuff would be parcelled higgledy-piggledy and taken to it's new, temporary site, a site chosen entirely at your discretion.'

'If the gallery and strong-room are empty, doesn't it suggest there's been a successful sale since the last police visit?' Harpur said. 'The items have gone. Sold? So, where's the cash? Could Jack point to credits of that magnitude in his bank statement?'

'I don't believe the police would have a right to demand such disclosure, would they, nor to search for currency in Darien? I say again, Jack wouldn't have been charged. What could he be charged with? Of course, things might go wrong. Whatever we try, that will be a possibility. We have to do what we can, and removal seems to me the least likely ploy to come unstuck.

'For example, you might opt for transfer of the items to some-where in your home. That could be all right, unless more is known about your hitch to Jack than we realize. Would Iles think it a brilliant chuckle-worthy dodge to point the searchers towards your place in Arthur Street?'

'No, Iles isn't like that.'

'Of course he's like that.'

'He's fond of a jape, admittedly, but that's all.'

'The japes he's fondest of do someone, or more than one, what he'd regard as hilarious damage. However, if you did choose your home, you'd need to be careful. Obviously, you would be unwise to hide these items at the back of an airing cupboard. They'd be unnoticeable, it's true. But the heat, the general atmos-phere of an airing cupboard could have unfavourable effects on the surface of some items, particularly very old items, which are likely to be the most valuable.

'Also, I gather you have children who will probably roam around the house and might not understand what these bundles were. Or, perhaps worse, *would* understand. And then we have the pretty undergraduate, Denise, part-time live-in, full of intel-ligent curiosity about parcels. Would you be able to satisfy her

– about the parcels, that is? Plus, I gather she's a smoker, so, fire risk.

'Or possibly you'd think of a furniture depository. Some risk of discovery or/and theft there. No depository would have insurance cover big enough for items of this value, possibly millions. Besides, Jack would probably not want to cough the kind of full-disclosure demanded by insurance companies because some of the items might have mysterious pasts which he'd like to keep mysterious. But, then, the whole stratagem is going to be chancy – we'll be talking risk and taking risk continually. I don't think a shed in the garden or on an allotment would do owing to damp and vermin. Jack would be able to advise on conservation matters.'

'No, don't do that.'

'Don't ask his opinion? He's very experienced in these things. But if you would rather no, all right and we—'

'I'm saying, don't approach Jack at all about a removal of items by me.'

'Oh?'

'No, impossible.'

'How so?'

'It's unthinkable, Alice.'

'Back a vehicle up to the kitchen door at Darien, load, drive to wherever you've selected. Maybe one journey, maybe two. Isn't it totally practical?'

'Perhaps it is, but it can't happen, Alice.'

'Can't? Why?'

'I'm sorry. Really. I can tell you've given it all a lot of thought.'

'I've plenty of time for that.' Pause. Possibly something between a sob and a groan. Then: 'You're afraid? You don't stand by your friends?'

So, he'd been right to expect the roots of an established matiness to get some hard light on them. 'No go, Alice. As I said, I'm the law. That would be a flagrant crime – perverting the course of justice, or some such.'

'Ah.'

'What?'

'I get it,' she said.

'What?'

The next bit from Alice came as a mid-Atlantic snarl, some

Eastwood (Clint) some east London (Peckham). '"Flagrant" is the problem, is it? You don't mind a more sly and furtive arrangement?'

'Sly', 'furtive', a fair description of informing. Harpur thought so, but didn't say so. 'The friendship has boundaries. That's always been the case.'

'And now you're being asked to move outside those boundaries – to give some actual, positive help in a possible crisis. This scares you, does it?'

'It's against the nature of things.'

'Which things? Which nature? Time and tide? The rotation of the earth?'

'The kind of contact between Jack and me.'

'It has to benefit you, you, exclusively you. Jack maybe – only maybe?'

'I hope it's good for both of us.'

'You hope!'

Harpur thought he might hear her bite and splinter the phone. She'd get docked privileges. He said, 'There's a complexity about it, a delicacy, which make it difficult for people outside this kind of life to understand. I'm not knocking you, Alice. Some magistrates and even judges can't plumb it intelligently. They think information should come to the police from clear, impeccable sources and by clear impeccable means, like getting the morning paper through the letterbox. The kind of good information we need is too precious and dangerous to arrive so easily. I have to be very subtle. And those who supply it have to be subtle as well.'

'I don't know about subtle. You sound pious and very, very guarded, Harpur, a bit like my US husband.'

Over the phone Harpur heard not any enraged munching of a receiver but the sound of a heavy door being opened. He silently rejoiced and tried to get a message to his sweat glands that stress might reduce shortly, thank God. A different female voice, not harsh or unkind, said, 'Time's up, Alice.'

'I can give you the private detective details, and that's all,' Harpur said at a rush. 'Got a pencil?'

THIRTY

After a minute Harpur replaced the receiver. It was a hesitant, gentle movement, no vehement, slam-bang, get stuffed, cut-off. Anyone watching and ignorant of the situation would probably read the sweet restraint all wrong. It could look as though Harpur yearned to keep contact with the other end of the line; hoped to prolong this precious link for a couple more moments before an absolute break.

A nice, stupid interpretation, of course. But Harpur did feel he shouldn't act as if delighted to silence Mrs Lamb at last, the chopsy, scheming old dear, even if he bloody well was. He had something not far from true sympathy for her and the way things had turned out: the holiday at Darien ruined by violence, then a trial, then jail. He wanted respite from her unforgiving mind and vocabulary, though. He certainly did not blame himself for taking her call, and would be ready to do it again, say some months on. Mrs Lamb's anxieties might have lessened by then.

Although that go-nowhere discussion closed, he had something else he needed to say, but not to Alice Lamb. He shifted from where he'd been sitting at his work station facing the computer screen, and felt more relaxed now in one of the room's two large, tan, leather easy chairs, relaxed and unbadgered. Superintendents and chief superintendents qualified for a couple of these, like school colours. Iles did better: as an assistant chief constable, he got three in his suite, plus a cheval mirror, to help him check his uniform when leaving for some glossy civic shindig. The cheval glass stood slim and oblong, fixed by swivel couplings in a mahogany frame, and could be tilted to allow a total inspection, head to foot. Iles kept it at an angle that avoided his Adam's apple, which he considered an ugly blight and an offence.

Harpur regarded himself as 'acutely furniture-sensitive'. Different kinds of chair, for instance, like this recent change, could produce very varied Harpur moods. For him, furniture was not neutral. It did more than passively provide a setting for action.

It was part of that action. He wondered sometimes whether any published research existed into the complex psychological clout of upholstery, cheval mirrors, chiffoniers, cushions, wardrobes, nests of tables, sofas, china cabinets. He wished he could ask Iles. It was the kind of thing the ACC might know. There wasn't much Iles *didn't* know, or couldn't make a brilliantly defiant pretense of knowing. But Harpur reckoned that if he mentioned the furniture topic Iles would kill it off fast. Most likely, he'd assume that Harpur had contracted some early middle-age mania and now hilariously believed he was an intellectual, a heavyweight abstract thinker. Iles would probably listen to Harpur's opening couple of words and reply, 'Go fuck yourself, Col,' or something less comradely. Harpur didn't ask.

Instead, his voice low – virtually a confidential whisper – he addressed Fate. This was something he did now and then, usually to protest about a particularly foul, relentless, bruising tumult of events. Hazel, his elder daughter, had told him that a belief in Fate was 'a measly opt-out from responsibility', but he had this habit all the same. Today he offered Fate only thorough gratitude: 'Thanks for intervening at that spot-on moment. By opening a door you shut out extra uncomfortable truths,' he said. Harpur felt pleased by that jokey play-about with words – opening something to shut it. Alice would probably have a grammar term for this. Not subjunctive.

She had hurt him. It angered Harpur that a convict of either gender could achieve that from behind bars. He disliked hearing the description of his understanding with Jack so damned accurately and mercilessly put. Harpur considered that some relationships should not be too thoroughly defined: informant and handler, for instance. All police forces were ordered to follow clear, specified rules for this kind of secret work. Not every detective and every informant tamely kowtowed, though. Harpur believed that, if there was something holding two people together, such as Jack and himself, let it prove this by successes, not by poncy, intelligent analysis and regulations.

Alice had told Harpur the informant arrangement 'has to benefit you, you, you. Jack maybe. Only maybe.' Correct? She hadn't used the word 'informant', but that's obviously what she was getting at. It made him feel disgustingly selfish and yellow:

someone who would abandon a buddy if it helped keep Harpur safe. The fact that much of this friendship was simply a crafty business fix didn't affect her view. She obviously thought pals owed each other support, regardless. She must believe Harpur was dodging out of that duty for fear of what might follow – follow for him, him, him, and his, his, his career.

About this Alice was essentially right, and he felt glad that the warder and the phone booth door had stopped any further painful, unnecessary frankness from her. Alice might have forgotten about tact and decorum through living in the States. She'd called him 'pious'. Perhaps that was fair. Hadn't he piously, big-headedly, told her he was the law, boom-boom? And for the law to be caught with God knew how many pictures of uncertain histories stashed away at home was a dire risk. He couldn't contemplate it.

But that exit line, escape line: 'Got a pencil?' he regretted – especially because it had been used twice, like a contemptuous chorus. It was so crudely final, so dismissive, so cruel. An anxious mother deserved some tenderness, despite this mother being Alice.

But, yes, she had brought a pencil and paper with her for the call. The prison officer had given her a minute to write the number down. 'I'll think about contacting the agency,' Alice said. 'Goodbye, Harpur. Talking to you has been a bummer.'

'Now then, Alice, we can do without that Yank coarse language,' the screw had said. 'This end there are standards to be kept up, if you don't mind.'

Hurriedly now, Harpur had said, 'Alice, I—'

THIRTY-ONE

B ut why always Harpur, hurried or not?
    Well, it wasn't always. Iles would often silence him with fairly poisonous put-downs. Harpur had to get some talk in when he could. Chances were not guaranteed.

THIRTY-TWO

Take that moment near the end of my funeral when Iles returned to his seat alongside Harpur – a short-stepped, slightly shuffling, dodgy knees approach back down the aisle, maybe for a moment to play-act harmlessness, diffidence, even humility. Normally, Iles didn't have much to do with those flagrantly unbombastic qualities, but perhaps he liked to confuse people now and then. He must have decided to mimic doddering frailty in what he considered a perfect setting: the non-denominational crem chapel. This would be after his nicely behaved session in the pulpit, and his polite chatter about me and my extinction with Judith and Daphne. Perhaps there were extremely brief interludes when he came to realize that everyone, including himself, was equally human and therefore deserved to be humanely treated. Obviously he couldn't stick for long with that equality notion or he wouldn't be Iles.

Harpur did manage to get out a mock-respectful, piss-taking tribute to Iles for his performance, claiming that it had 'graced' the congregation. 'Graced!' Oh, God! I'm pretty certain it was 'graced' not 'greased'. Hard to associate Iles with grace, though, except as part of a kick-in-the-balls send-up. Amazing grace? The whole exchange between Harpur and Iles at this point was reasonably audible. It took place during a pause in the proceedings while Bainbridge Williamson made for the pulpit to give the second eulogy.

And how did the assistant chief reply to Harpur? I have that verbatim: it's the sort of come-back that does stay ugly and exact in the memory. 'Just don't fuck up, you jerk, now there's some extra material, that's all.' Naturally, the harmlessness, diffidence and humility had been locked back into their hutch by then. Those two unholy, hard 'ck' and 'k' words with their insolent vowel sounds, gave the Iles response a savage start, dishing out enmity like a champ's old one-two. At the agency we had occasional contact with the police on some cases, and

I knew this kind of morale-boost priming of Harpur by Iles was standard, ending the possibility of any further conversation for a while. Also, there had been that affair mentioned by Iles involving his wife and Harpur[7] which might account for some of Iles's acute mellowness deficit at times. It was widely known about, and often featured in an agonized screaming fit from Iles, a full-voice, public screaming fit. His reference to it at the funeral wasn't anywhere near that pitch, though. And no rage spit flew.

So, what 'extra material' did the ACC have in mind? Mainly, of course, it was the claim by both women in turn, Judith and Daphne, that Judith had been the cause, or at least *a* cause, of my death. Judith had put it simply, hadn't she? Again, I have the words right, I think. Standing in the aisle she'd said, 'I might have helped put an end to that life.' By 'that life' she meant me, mine. Her confession had immediately followed a slab of production-line triteness from Iles arguing that the funeral was not only communal mourning but also celebrated a life, i.e.,Thomas Wells Hart's. I could have preferred a different way to celebrate my life, such as letting it go on, not prematurely having it end up here casketted. But that option wasn't offered. I think of that poem about the fallen in the Great War: 'They shall not grow old as we that are left grow old: Age shall not weary them, nor the years condemn.'

But most probably they would have *liked* to grow old even if the extra years brought a bit of weariness and tooth loss.

Not long after the Iles lyric, Daphne Davenpole had given a special reason – special to her – for accusing Judith of getting me killed. It was Judith's 'disgraceful appetite' – sexual appetite – according to Daphne, who, personally, and in opposition, was all for decency and rectitude. Because of Judith, Daphne said, I had fallen into a job at the Righton agency, and with it the pretty chance to die violently and young.

When Iles in his bracing manner told Harpur at the funeral not to fuck up, he probably meant that between them the two women – and especially Judith – between them the pair undoubtedly had the kind of private information that showed why and

7 See most earlier books in the series

how I had to die. Iles wanted it. Harpur had better come up with it.

What would he discover if he now dealt with these new possibilities in the unfucked-up style Iles fancied so much? I thought I could see one direction Harpur might choose. Because I'd come to regard Judith's anxieties as possibly justified, I told her about what I regarded as an interesting few developments to do with the art situation and, possibly, her brother. She might want to pass some of this or all of it on to Harpur, if he interviewed her – interviewed her again, that is: he'd already had a brief talk with her after the Cairn Close shooting.

Outlining things for her, I said that soon after I'd arrived for work at the Righton agency one Tuesday morning Bainbridge Williamson rang on the internal and asked me to go to see him in his office. This was a large, super-tidy room upstairs. He didn't go much on work stations and computers and, instead, had an ancient, large roll-top desk and a secretary's soft-seat, revolving, armless chair for when he was working at it. He could swing around to deal with interviews and meetings in the room. There were half a dozen chintzy armchairs for guests.

Watercolour portraits of his first-back-to-the-loft racing pigeons crowded two of the walls. They'd been done for him at a couple of hundred quid a time, frame included, by an artistic member of the pigeon club where Bainbridge chaired the management committee. He'd told me that he and the artist both saw obvious facial differences between the birds and would be able to recognize any one of them flying low or pecking at a lawn. I suppose this identification element made it a suitable kind of hobby for a detective, though to me they were indistinguishable as pictures, and would be also as part of a flock in the air or on the ground. This wasn't the kind of thing to tell Bainbridge, though. It would be hurtful. He'd been attracted to the sport, apparently, by *The Day Of The Jackal* film where the chief French detective is called away from his back garden pigeon loft to hunt a hitman plotting to kill de Gaulle. There's a touch of symbolism, maybe, though I didn't see it very clearly: the pigeon has to find its way home, often covering huge distances, and the detective has to find his way to the jackal fast. The captioned names of some of the birds could possibly have a bearing on the private detective career:

Discovery, True Grit, Venture, Dauntless. 'Look at the questing nature of Discovery's eyes, yet not without some sly humour,' Bainbridge had trilled to me one day. 'And a kind of warrior boldness in the beak and jaws of Dauntless.' I could imagine Dauntless being late back from a flight across Europe and Bainbridge getting in touch with Interpol to ask about any sightings of a pigeon with a gung-ho beak. Bainbridge's loft was on a balcony at the rear of the Righton building.

I went up to the second floor and found he had a guest, a woman, not one I recognized. I reckoned she'd be in her early thirties. She was black and wore a brilliantly cut, navy pin-striped trouser suit, the jacket over a crimson silk shirt or blouse with a bound scoop neckline. She had what I took to be a gold signet ring on the index finger of her right hand and a small, glinting opal brooch on her left lapel. It was an ensemble as cleverly and imaginatively planned as anything I had ever seen in Righton, staff or client. OK, this was not saying much, but it was worth saying just the same. She looked as though she could have been on her way to a company directors' meeting somewhere and had just happened to drop in to see small fry Bainbridge and smaller fry me *en route*.

Her hair had been cut to just above shoulder length, encircling a squarish, friendly, guarded face. Her 'hello' when Bainbridge introduced us was also friendly and guarded. I'd become used to Righton's visitors appearing guarded. They had troubles; wouldn't be here, otherwise, and they'd be wondering whether Righton could help and how much it would cost whether Righton could or failed to. The friendliness from this morning's visitor was a bonus – so far, anyway.

She stood to greet me. She was about 5' 8" on medium heels, slim, straight backed, perhaps athletic when a little younger, could be the high-jump or javelin. We shook hands. She had long, shapely fingers. I could visualize them cosseting a javelin shaft pre a first-rate chuck. Her shoulders were neat, not bulky, but I thought I sensed big, steroid-free strength there. Bainbridge said her name was Enid Aust.

'Enid is here not on her own account, Tom, but as what might be called an intermediary, I suppose,' Bainbridge said. He had spun his chair around from the desk to talk to us. She and I took easy chairs now. 'Yes, Enid hopes that between the three of us we can see to the rather urgent wishes of one of her colleagues,' he said.

'Well, an *ex*-colleague,' Enid said, with a good smile. 'I'm out. Have been for a week. Alice is still inside. It'll be a while yet.'

'Alice Lamb, Tom,' Bainbridge said.

'We had a sort of affinity,' Enid said. 'This was more than just neighbourly cells. We'd both shot someone, killed someone, but in a good cause. Mine was family. These things can happen. In a way, Alice's experience was similar. She needed to protect someone – family, too – felt a duty to protect someone. The someone is who I'm here to discuss, isn't it?' She paused, frowned, pursed her lips. 'Oh, I ask isn't it, but you don't know why I'm here, do you, Tom? Presumptuous of me to rush on like that.'

'Enid had our number from Colin Harpur, via Alice,' Bainbridge said.

'Not that it's secret,' Enid said. 'Alice could have rung. We were granted the phone vouchers. But she thought it would be better if things were talked over face to face rather than like that . . . So, here's my face. And now there's your two faces, so we are face-to-face-to-face.'

'Tom does a lot of our investigations,' Bainbridge replied. 'I wanted him in on the conversation.'

'Alice would be grateful for anyone who can act on her behalf,' Enid replied. 'This Harpur, the cop, talked to her but he couldn't do much, or so he said. Protocol. Well, maybe. Except he sort of invited her to take things further by giving the phone number. A kind of prompt. I'm prompted, as you see. Harpur obviously trusts you. This probably impressed Alice. I felt obliged to help.

'Perhaps you'll think that a closeness based on homicides has something negative and dubious about it, but remember Bonnie and Clyde. We're blood sisters, Alice and I. We have a sort of mutual support contract that will still link us even when she gets out in three years and eight months if she can keep up the good behaviour, and she's not too bad at that. They'll miss her teaching the reading and writing, though.'

'Tom, Alice worries about her son,' Bainbridge said.

'She feels responsible,' Enid said. 'She wanted to help, tried to help, and it all turned rotten. Guilt. Two loads of it – one decided by the jury, the other decided by herself. She's plagued by conscience is our Alice. She might seem breezy and free-wheeling but there's a lot of depth, too, a lot of motherly concern. Me, I copped guilt in the court, too, but I never blamed myself. That would have seemed illogical – one crime, one punishment, and anything additional unjust. I've tried to talk Alice into seeing things that way, but she's got this sort of puritan streak.'

Her tone said Alice's self-punishment was crazy, but it also hinted at admiration: Alice wouldn't try to dodge blame. I had the feeling Enid would do anything she could to put matters right for Alice, or as right as they could be put. 'Alice wanted Harpur to hide some of the works in his home, but he wasn't having that,' Enid said. 'I can see why it might not be to the point, anyway. She's scared someone, or a gang, is going to do a break-in at Darien, attracted by the publicity for that first attack. Jack told her on a visit that he'd already had someone – someone possibly dangerous – scouting around at the house. But to move the pics secretly to Harpur's place or anywhere else isn't going to stop the second attempt, is it? The raiders couldn't know the gallery had been cleared and would go ahead. Jack Lamb is going to be in just as much peril, maybe more. The burglars would be very pissed off. But they might guess what had happened and knock Lamb about to force the new address out of him.'

Enid sounded like someone used to planning and organizing. She could do the for and against arguments in an easy, methodical fashion, though in this case almost all her arguments were against.

'Harpur would have to beware of too much involvement,' Bainbridge said.

'Alice was disappointed in him, very,' Enid said. 'She seemed to think there was a particular link between Harpur and her son, and that this would come into play. She thought he'd want to help Jack Lamb – as a senior cop but also as a pal. But she didn't clarify. I wanted to know, what kind of particular link. She kept it all a bit vague, though.'

'Well, yes, Alice would,' Bainbridge said.

'But why?' she said.

'That's how these things operate,' Bainbridge said.

'What are we talking about?' Enid said.

'He'd need to move very carefully, if at all,' Bainbridge replied, except it didn't seem to be a reply, or not to her question. 'But, yes, a certain kind of relationship might exist. I've sometimes wondered.'

'Gay?' Enid said.

'No.'

'What, then?' Enid said.

'It's a very subtle exercise Harpur runs,' Bainbridge said.

'Which exercise?' she said.

'Hiding the pics at his place would take things too far. That would be not at all subtle,' Bainbridge said.

'Which things?' she replied. She turned to me. 'Do *you* understand which things, Tom?'

'Tom's comparatively new to this trade,' Bainbridge said.

'Ah! Oh! I believe I understand now. With a bit of silly melodrama Enid put a hand over her mouth and began to whisper. 'We're in the area of cloudy nod-and-wink, are we? Only those who've been around for a decade or two get to be told. That would seem to mean . . .' She ended the theatricals and dropped her hand. She spoke normally. 'Look, Bainbridge, are you talking about touting, informing, finking?' she asked. 'Lamb feeds Harpur?'

I'd decided myself that this was what the hints from Bainbridge might mean, but I wouldn't have had the cheek to ask. He'd have his reasons for keeping things vague. But tact had no hold on Enid.

'He's got teenage daughters, intelligent kids, full of curiosity. And there's a part live-in girlfriend, an undergraduate up the road. Another brain around the house. What chance of hiding a stack of pics, even if out of their frames?' Bainbridge said.

'You think Harpur would be afraid villains might discover he did special favours for Lamb, and so kaput to the snitch service – that's apart from Harpur having his house burgled in search of the art?' Enid said. 'And maybe the kids and his girlfriend clobbered, or worse? He's in the phone book, I gather. Easily located.'

'Would Lamb agree for the items to be moved, anyway?' Bainbridge said. 'Unlikely. They're his wealth, his capital, his

social status, his manhood, still valuable even if the prices fell
a bit. He's used to having works of the great around his property,
some of them quite possibly genuine and reeking with aura. He
can rub shoulders with Chagall and Bocklin. He'd miss them too
much. He might trust Harpur – almost certainly does – but, as
you say, Enid, he couldn't rely on the children and the girlfriend
to stay silent if they came across the works hidden away, but not
hidden away well enough.'

Of course, I thought about saying that I'd gone out to have a
look at Darien some while ago and saw the approach of the van
and so on, plus later, the van in the lay-by and my baffling
conversation with the unknown woman. But I didn't see that this
would take us very much further on. I hadn't mentioned it to
Bainbridge at the time: the trip wasn't a Righton job, just personal
curiosity because of Judith. I was, and still would be, very tight-
fisted with any discoveries I made. I know why. Although the
private detective course Bainbridge had sent me on covered a lot
of the trade's skills, I'd also picked up there what Enid might
have called the nod-and-wink message, an unspoken, but very
present and pervasive theme. It was that information might be
immensely precious and should never get casually passed on to
others unless advantageously needed; not even to allies, friends
and work mates. After all, it's fitting for a private detective to
be private, and for a private eye to see things he/she might not
let others see. Let's adjust the childhood jingle: *'I spy with my
little eye something beginning with confidentiality, and maybe
staying like that . . .'*

'Alice has money,' Enid said. 'She can cope with your fees.
There was a good divorce settlement in the States. Her husband
built a fortune and knew how to look after it – at least until
Alice's lawyers got going. And I'm all right for cash: family
boodle that came my way despite the shooting – or some would
say *because* of it. I can help if required. That's the kind of buddies
we are. Jail has some positives, you see.'

'*The Pilgrim's Progress* written in prison and *The Ballade of
Reading Gaol* written *about* it. But also *Mein Kampf* is a choky
book,' Bainbridge said. 'You're talking about continuous protection, are you?'

'That's what Alice wants, at least short term,' Enid replied.

'The cop, Harpur, obviously believes you can do it, and do it well.'

'The agency couldn't undertake that kind of commission unless the subject of it – Lamb, in this case – agreed,' Bainbridge said. 'This is not like covert surveillance where the agency operatives act without permission, of course, and, if possible, secretly. We'd need authorization and cooperation. It would be a kind of imposition, a kind of stalking, otherwise.'

'We understand that, Alice and I,' Enid said. 'What she wants is someone from the agency to go with me to see Jack Lamb and let him know what his mother wishes and if possible persuade him to accept. She's tried talking to him along those lines, naturally. It didn't work. She would like an outsider to confirm to Jack that her worries are reasonable and have to be dealt with urgently. *How* to deal with them can be worked out later – but not too much later. The objective now, though, is to convince him that he and the girl he lives with and his collection are not safe.'

'Oh, this sounds very practical and possible,' Bainbridge said. 'Tom could certainly accompany you for that kind of meeting with Lamb.'

'Pleased to,' I said, and I think more or less meant it.

THIRTY-THREE

'**G**ot a pencil?' Memory of the blurted question – questions – still made Harpur disgusted with himself. They had been a brush-off. They tried to reduce things to a bit of clerking. He'd longed to escape from Alice Lamb's voice and loud cleverness, so he'd manufactured a chance. 'Got a pencil?' The words glittered with indifference. They'd told her, without actually telling her, kindly to get lost behind a heavy steel door.

When he hindsighted all this next day, it struck him as heartless and slippery. Untypical? He hoped it was. He decided he must do something to show he wasn't an arrogant, uncaring, treacherous twerp. He needed this correction. It might soothe his conscience. Normally, Harpur could keep his conscience reasonably well dungeoned, only rarely let out and then on a very short chain. To be bothered so much by it now puzzled him.

'What's wrong, Dad?' Jill said.

His daughters were very good at spotting changes of mood in Harpur, and tireless in trying to find what caused them. 'Wrong?' he said. 'Why should anything be wrong?'

'Because something is,' Jill said. Harpur and the two girls were talking in the big Arthur Street sitting room, the TV silent but showing a soccer match.

'Is it to do with Denise?' Hazel said.

'Is what to do with Denise?' Harpur replied.

'The anxiety,' Jill said. 'The suffering.'

'Which anxiety?' he said 'Which suffering?'

'Yours,' Hazel said. 'We've discussed it, Jill and I.'

'Do you worry about her lungs?' Jill said.

'Lungs?' Harpur said.

'The smoking,' Jill said. 'We had that medical lecture at school with pictures of a smoker's lungs. Like old bath mats. How many Marlborough a day? She doesn't seem to care. It's a known fact that although men are cutting down on their smoking, girls aren't. In a way, it's very nice that you *are* worried about her, because it shows you really love her, which, obviously, would include her lungs, not just her outer body, the various aspects of it. Don't you ever say to her that she shouldn't do so many ciggies? She plays lacrosse for the uni with a lot of flinging and dashes, so she needs bags of breath, but can her lungs give her enough?'

'She's an adult,' Hazel said. 'She has to make her own choices. Dad can't live her life for her. The warning's on the packets. She can read.'

'But he could tell her that he wants her life to go on and on, which it might not if she's always sucking in these loads of tar.'

'I have to go out,' Harpur said.

'Or you might very reasonably be concerned about the age gap,' Hazel replied.

'Which?' Harpur said.

'She's not twenty and you're nearly forty,' Hazel said.

'Dad's only thirty-seven,' Jill said.

'Yes, nearly forty,' Hazel said.

'That doesn't bother her,' Harpur said.

'The age gap has always been there,' Jill said. 'Why should he get upset about it now?'

'She's with young people including men most of the time at the uni,' Hazel said. 'They're reading poetry full of stuff about romance and intimacy.'

'So what?' Jill said.

'It could make students think along the same lines,' Hazel said.

'She loves Dad,' Jill said. 'She doesn't have to fancy men students just because they're the same age as herself and getting turned on by literature. Think of that film star on the movie channel sometimes – supposed to be funny – Charlie Chaplin. He had a girlfriend much younger than himself.'

'And nearly got sent to jail for it,' Hazel said.

'But, like you said, Haze, Denise is an adult. Dad's not a what-you-call-it. A paedo.'

'Do you know how I see things, Dad?' Hazel replied.

'Which things?' Harpur said.

'You and Denise. I mean, where's it going?' Hazel said.

'Does it have to go anywhere?' Harpur said. 'It's the present. It's now. That will do, won't it? She's off to see a French movie called *Tip Top* in the university Film Society. She'll come here afterwards. I'll be busy elsewhere for an hour or so.'

'Haze means what about the future, I think,' Jill said.

'Denise keeps a distance,' Hazel replied.

'But she stays here very often,' Harpur said.

'Yes, very often. But she doesn't stay here *only*. She's got that flat or room in the student block, Jonson Court, Jonson without an h. I don't think she wants to be here all the time in case it seems like she's our stepmother, although only nineteen. That's why I asked where it's going, the relationship. It's a lovely relationship and we're always pleased for her to be here, but what next?'

To Harpur it seemed another instance of wanting a definition where it might be much more comfortable without. He would have liked something permanent. He and Denise had talked about it once or twice. Once. He could see she wasn't ready for that. The topic had faded.

'Denise always has one life in sort of reserve,' Hazel said.

'I don't understand that, Haze,' Jill said.

'A main life and a sort of backup. 'I don't know which we are, important or on the side. So, just think of tonight: she choosing one way – to the cinema – and you disappear *elsewhere*, destination unknown, separate existences.'

'Denise asked me to go to the Film Society with her,' Harpur replied.

'She knew you'd turn it down. Foreign picture, a bit high-falutin, in your opinion. I've heard of the film. It has the great actress Isabelle Huppert in it as a detective.'

'You won't say any of this, well . . . very *difficult* stuff to Denise, will you, Haze?' Jill said.

'Of course not,' Hazel said. 'Denise is great, no question. But I was just wondering what's what?'

'I'll make a move,' Harpur replied.

'Is this to do with what's been niggling you?' Hazel said. 'Can you put it right in just an hour?'

'Put what right?' Harpur said.

'Whatever it is that's niggling you,' Hazel said.

'Who says something is niggling me?' Harpur said.

'Jill and I,' Hazel replied.

And he recognized that they had it right. When it came to guessing how he felt this day or that they usually did get it right, though not the cause. They couldn't know about his blundering interview with Alice Lamb, his regrets, and his fairly useless urge to do something about them.

As promised, he meant to order increased patrolling around Darien, very soon. But, of course, Iles would have to be notified of such a change in duties. Harpur didn't want participation from anyone else yet. He saw this mission as a kind of apology. It had to come from him personally and, in the first instance, at least, him, very solo. He'd have a little tour of the Darien area himself. He assumed that if there was going to be trouble it would happen at night, so he'd double the patrol surveillance between 9 p.m. and 6 a.m. and he was setting out tonight at just before 10 p.m. to do what he could to match these conditions.

Denise had a key and Harpur's daughters might still be up, anyway, when she arrived. He thought an hour could be an over-estimate for his trip. It would not be much more than a gesture, a gesture aimed only at him, but crucial – for him. Jill would probably understand why he felt like this. Hazel would probably understand, too, but would regard it as weak, sloppy and illogical. Hazel was strong on logic.

THIRTY-FOUR

Harpur drove towards Lamb's country house and estate, Darien, a few miles from the city. It stood in just over four acres at the foot of a wooded hillock. Quite a few people who ran dodgy, or more than dodgy, businesses liked to live somewhere non-urban, spacious, sedate, with plenty of manageable greenery, a shoe-scraper at the front door, durable trees and restful views. For instance, from *Darien*, Jack could just see the plentiful chimneys of Low Pastures, fine home of Ralph Ember, club owner and brilliantly successful wholesaler of most recreational substances, often referred to – though not in his presence – as Panicking Ralph or Panicking Ralphy, on account of some alleged disastrous chicken moment in his past.[8]

Darien's notable history was an extra, unique factor that had persuaded Jack to buy. From occasional visits on the quiet for confidential talks with Lamb, Harpur knew the layout well. But last time it was an official call as top detective after Jack's mother shot and killed an intruder. The property had seven bedrooms and looked out over a small lake, then agricultural land and, in the far distance, a stretch of coastline and the sea. Two of the original five reception rooms downstairs had been knocked into one to create a gallery, and there was a strongroom in the basement. The main downstairs room was panelled in mahogany and had a minstrel's gallery. From there a couple of times on a mouth organ Jack had played 'Keep The Home Fires Burning' and other First World War songs while Harpur listened below.

During the seventeenth-century British civil war that led to the execution of Charles I, the house apparently served as a Royalist outpost. This thrilled Jack, though not because it took the king's side: he'd have been just as delighted if the then owner favoured Cromwell's Roundheads. What excited Lamb was the notion of a thoroughly documented link with serious military disputes and violence, and the fortunes of battle. Soldiering fascinated Jack. He'd never enlisted but possessed a fine and constantly growing collection of international army surplus uniforms. His meetings with Harpur weren't always at Darien and often when he arrived at some rendezvous spot outside with fresh tip-offs, he might be wearing a French peaked kepi, German SS tunic and Scottish regimental kilt, or a British bum-freezer short overcoat that rested on the mounted officer's saddle, when cavalry meant horses, not tanks.

Now and then Jack spoke glowingly of 'the soldier's art', which apparently was a quote from somewhere. He'd explained to Harpur that this 'art' wasn't to do with pictures but with a fundamental tactic adopted by troops – 'think first, fight afterwards'.

Jack reckoned parts of Darien were Elizabethan, but plenty of rebuilding and extensions had taken place in what he said was a 'Georgian style': five, narrow, vertical windows in the front upstairs; four downstairs leaving space between two pairs for the door; a stone porch or portico; a coach house converted into garages and stables. There was a wide, gravelled, larch-lined slightly curving drive that opened through high metal gates on to a minor road. Harpur intended doing a slow, circular tour around the house and grounds, a couple of ten-minute pauses with the car lights off and the engine cut, then, if everything looked all right, as he expected, a quick return to Arthur Street. It would add up to a token episode of surveillance, that was all.

During the second of these observation pauses, though, while he was parked just outside the gates, Harpur thought he saw movement in the grounds, not far from the adapted coach house. Or movements. Possibly two people. He had a pair of night-view field glasses in the glove compartment and brought these out now and looked for any more activity. Nothing. Perhaps even if he'd been successful it would have meant nothing, anyway. It was dark but not terribly late and Jack might be out in the grounds, perhaps taking a stroll with his girlfriend, Helen, before turning in. But Harpur did think there had been a kind of scurrying element in what he'd seen, something furtive and hurried and purposeful.

While Harpur still had the night glasses aimed at where he'd glimpsed the two figures – *thought* he'd glimpsed the two figures – a gross, grotesquely distorted, blurred face intervened at the far end of the binoculars. It blotted out Harpur's view of the lake area, and of anything else except the vastly off-putting sight of an over-magnified farrargo of human features. It seemed to be within an inch or two of the lenses: a total disruptive take-over. To read any expression in the various fleshly lumps, outcrops and fronds would be impossible, and madness to try; or even to search for evidence of a settled, feasible shape, an identity.

What might almost certainly be a pair of lips appeared briefly in this multi-coloured hotchpotch and then, after a few moments of swirl, eddy, flux and wobble, formed themselves into what was now definitely a pair of fully functional lips, obviously made for communication, and/or food and possibly for whistling. Harpur saw very credible intimations of a nose just above them. The lips seemed to aim themselves at Harpur and spoke; spoke loudly enough to get through the side window of his car. They said conversationally, 'What ho! Col.'

Harpur lowered the glasses and put them away. He opened the driver's side door. The interior light came on automatically and was enough to reach out and show Iles and a woman Harpur didn't recognize. The assistant chief wore a hip-length, navy donkey jacket over a black roll-top sweater, a crimson scarf, jeans, walking boots, and a tan coloured, woollen bobble hat. The woman would be in her late forties and had on a four-pocketed, waterproof jacket with a grey faux fur collar, black moleskin trousers pushed into short-legged brown wellington boots, and a beige, woollen balaclava helmet.

'Naturally, even before we got close enough for me to recognize the car, I wondered if it was you doing a slow circuit of the house and surrounds, Harpur,' Iles said. 'I couldn't see what might be the objective, but I felt extremely confident that you'd have your reasons, not necessarily sane reasons, but reasons. I remarked about it to Pamela, didn't I, Pam? I said approximately, "This will be Colin Harpur, a quaint but occasionally effective member of our middle management, on some sort of secret prowl. He'll have his reasons, but whether he'll disclose them, or disclose them truthfully, is problematical. As the prophet asks: 'can the

Ethiopian change his skin or the leopard its spots?'– not that the
Ethiopan would want to change his skin in these anti-racist days
– a rhetorical question with the answer 'no' built in?'"

'Was it you two scampering about up near the one-time coach
house, now stables and garages, sir?' Harpur said.

'The thing about Jack Lamb is that he obviously can't have
alarms and CCTV fitted in case they get activated and bring the
law and order boys and girls out here again, you at their head,
Col, nosing around inside,' Iles replied.

'Where's your vehicle?' Harpur said.

'I didn't consider it wise in the circumstances to have Pam
wandering about here solo, no matter how fond of nature she
might be,' Iles replied.

'Which circumstances?' Harpur asked.

'I agreed at once when she asked for local help, as you can
understand, I'm sure, Col.'

Pam, standing a little behind Iles, had a torch. She lit up the
gates with it, and a blue plaque fixed on one of them. 'Something
written there,' she said and leaned forward for a closer view. 'It's
a Latin tag.' She read aloud: '"*Omnes Eodem Cogimur*", meaning,
I'd say, something like, "We are all shoved in the same direction."
That seems to cover the way we've met here tonight. Is Lamb a
scholar? I don't think his dossier mentions that.'

'Good old Horace,' Iles said. 'He had a nice flinty outlook.
You'll ask who is my companion, Col?'

'Who is your companion, sir?' Harpur said.

'Lamb would be puzzled if he knew about this night-time
colloquium gathering spontaneously at the entrance to his realm,
even if we *are* all shoved in the same direction,' Iles replied.

'It wasn't my intention to hang about for very long,' Harpur
said.

'No, I expect you've got something nice and amenable waiting
for you under the duvet in Arthur Street,' Iles said. 'Col's
extremely conscious of his social responsibilities, Pam, and keeps
markedly close ties with tertiary education and the local university
through an undergraduate called Denise. She is very safely above
the age of consent, which some people believe is set too high,
anyway.' Iles paused, then formed those lips to produce a
quavering, malign hiss. 'Col is even more safely above the age

of consent. My wife could confirm that some while before Denise if—'

'I feel inhospitable talking like this when you are standing in the cold,' Harpur said. 'You should get into the car.'

Iles said, 'Do you think I want to get into a car that you might have used for your disgraceful—?'

'Which dossier?' Harpur replied.

'Dossier?' Iles said.

'Pamela mentioned a dossier – Jack Lamb's dossier,' Harpur said.

'I'm with the national arts and antiques team in London,' she said. 'As you'd expect Lamb has come to our notice, if only because of the shooting. Actually, it's not *only* because of the shooting.'

'Pam and I worked together on some cases when I was in the Met,' Iles said. 'We've kept in touch. Pamela Venning. She and colleagues believe there's been something big and potentially nefarious for at least months on our ground, Col. She wanted a discreet scan of Lamb's place. So it needed to be night.'

'What big and potentially nefarious thing under way on our ground for at least months?' Harpur replied.

'*Only* potential. Col's offended, Pam. He's supposed to notice anything nefarious. But Pam's a specialist. She's handled some very large art-world cases,' Iles said. 'She's bound to be a bit ahead in this kind of case. Please don't feel any more superfluous than usual, Harpur.'

'I don't think I *am* ahead,' Pam said. 'He's out here, casing Lamb's place, isn't he? Lying doggo, lights and engine off so he can watch and not be watched. Routine skills. That signifies he knows something, perhaps the same kind of thing that I know, or half know.'

'Which kind is that?' Harpur replied.

'The kind you don't want to talk about,' Iles said. 'This would amount to several wagon-loads. Harpur generally comes at situations from some weird personal angle which by the fluke of flukes might now and then pay off. But you, Pam, you are the naturally gifted and educated expert.'

'Oh, yes, Colin,' she said. 'If anyone were made for such work it is emphatically and incontrovertibly I.'

Harpur found it unsettling to be addressed with terrific intensity by a woman wearing a balaclava, and who could do Latin. He associated balaclavas with Arctic exploration, usually by men, or old fashioned bank hold-ups. Her judderingly correct grammar – the 'I' rather than 'me' – also troubled him.

'I detest art, you see,' she said enthusiastically. 'It began as a suspicion but grew into a whole-hearted, healthy revulsion.'

'Oh?' Harpur replied. 'All art? Jack Lamb is a great fan of what he calls "the soldier's art".'

'Ah, Browning, and later the title of a novel by Anthony Powell. But Col is looking puzzled,' Iles said, with a merry, sympathetic chuckle, the hiss gone from his wordage now. 'Pam doesn't mean some particular painting or sculpture, nor the work of a particular school of artists.'

'It's the whole fucking brouhaha,' Pamela said.

'Pamela has often spoken to me in disgust about the whole fucking brouhaha,' Iles said. 'I'm not sure whether she overstates things, though. Occasionally a brouhaha is justified.'

'My mother always maintained that what Baden-Powell, creator of the boy scout movement, actually preached as a life-guide was not simply "Be prepared", but "Be prepared for brouhahas,"' Harpur replied. 'Over the years, though, the latter part fell away because few boys knew what a brouhaha was.'

'When I speak of a brouhaha I'm not referring merely to the kind of ludicrous and creepily reverend attitude towards canvases or stone or brass. What I object to goes deeper, so much deeper. I ask, "Why art at all?"' Pamela stated.

'In many ways this is merely a short, formal reconnaissance,' Harpur replied. 'Lamb had notorious trouble at Darien and occasionally I feel I should come out and take a quick squint in case of aftermath.'

'Art in its various fashions seeks to represent the real,' Pamela said. 'But why take the trouble when the real is already there? Isn't it grossly presumptuous, flagrantly unnecessary, to reduce the actual and active to something two dimensional and confined in a ghastly frame or stuck radiantly inanimate on a plinth? Wouldn't you say it's otiose, Col?'

'Some like it otiose,' Iles said.

'Serving no useful purpose,' Pam said. 'My thinking you see,

Colin, makes me a natural for this job. I'm not concerned about
the supposed aesthetic qualities of this or that piece of work. I
deal in its data: measurements, the type and colour of frame, its
dates and recorded history, and, in the case of sculpts, its weight.
These examples of supposed spectacular beauty are to me simply
items, and I deal with them – or more likely with their absence
– just as officers from a different squad would deal with burglary
losses, robbery losses, mugging losses, pickpocketing losses,
fraud losses. If alleged experts or auction records tell me this
picture of a chubby looking, sullen Dutch girl holding a pooch
is worth so many millions I will give a polite nod to show I've
heard what was said and as soon as is convenient discard that
information as . . . as, yes, otiose. I'll listen to chat about tints,
perspective and vigour in a job by Velasquez then get quickly
out of sight and throw up. Integrity is my watchword, Colin. My
family is famed for that going right back in history?'

'Integrity?' Harpur asked.

'Watchwords,' she said.

'Pam's going to be on our ground for some while, I think,
Harpur,' Iles said. 'She believes she might be closing in on some
exceptionally renowned items.'

'If I get some luck,' she replied. She gave a slight wave of
her hand which still held the torch, but unlit. Harpur sensed that
she meant to plead modesty by this gesture, a sort of, Oh, shucks,
please don't make me sound some sort of ace investigator. She
turned towards him 'Do I gather, Mr Harpur, that you saw
someone, or thought you saw someone, or maybe more than one,
close to the stables?'

'In that area,' Harpur said.

'It wouldn't have been Des and me,' Pamela said. 'I wanted
to have a look at the frontage of the main building and the
approach to it on the drive.'

'There's someone else here?' Iles said. He glanced about.

'Perhaps Jack and his girlfriend enjoying an evening walk in
the grounds,' Harpur said.

'Perhaps,' Pam replied.

'I wasn't certain I'd seen anyone at all,' Harpur said.

'It's interesting, though,' Pamela said.

'Perhaps,' Harpur said.

'Col's very open-minded,' Iles replied. 'Well, who'd want to get locked in with a mind like his?'

When Harpur reached home, the children were still up and Denise had arrived from the cinema. They were watching a world championship middleweight bout from the United States. Jill knew a lot about boxing. One of her favourite books was *The Sweet Science,* by A.J. Liebling, once a boxing writer for the *New Yorker* magazine. She'd asked for that one to be kept when Harpur had cleared the sitting room of his wife's learned and academic books and the shelving after her murder at the railway station car park.[9]

'You told us you'd be only an hour,' Hazel said.

'We thought we'd better wait up to see you were OK, Dad,' Jill said. 'It can be pretty hostile out there.'

'Hark at her!' Hazel said.

'Some complications delayed me,' Harpur said.

'What complications?' Jill said. 'I don't know what it means – complications. Is it like sudden difficulties?'

'You don't need "like",' Harpur said.

'You mean I don't need "like" because it wasn't just *like* sudden difficulties, it *was* sudden difficulties? So, what *were* these sudden difficulties? Were they so sudden that it took you a long time to deal with them owing to being not ready and prepared, which made you later than you'd expected?'

'What sort of thing was it, anyway, never mind the complications,' Hazel said. 'We don't expect you to cough the lot, but some ballpark indication.'

'What's that?' Jill said.

'What?' Hazel replied.

'A ballpark indication,' Jill said.

'I'm asking, which general type of police work – grievous bodily harm, drugs, terrorism, burglary?' Hazel said.

'In a park?' Jill asked.

'A ballpark as signifying a department in police work, without demanding too much detail.'

'I don't see how a park can be a department,' Jill replied.

'No, I don't suppose you can,' Hazel said.

9 See *Roses, Roses*

'Very much a formality only,' Harpur said.

'Someone of your rank going out at night for a formality?' Hazel said.

'People of my rank have a lot to do with formalities,' Harpur said. 'We've left the nitty-gritty behind.'

'These sudden complications are not to do with the nitty-gritty, is that right?' Jill asked.

'But these complications are to do with the formality?' Hazel said.

'Several people, including, obviously, myself had the same sort of purpose and we met.'

'They're all concerned with the formality?' Hazel said.

'It might be a formality for Dad, but not for the others, or not so much. This is how the complications would start,' Jill said.

'Met where?' Hazel asked.

'I don't think anyone learned very much,' Harpur replied.

'Neither do we,' Hazel said. There was a knock down and the boxing finished.

'Denise has been telling us about the film,' Jill said.

'To do with an informant,' Hazel said.

'Violent,' Denise said. 'But funny.'

'That's how films and stories should be,' Harpur said.

'It was in French, but Denise could understand the jokes because of her studies,' Jill said. 'She knows all kinds of French poems. There's one to do with the battle of Waterloo which Wellington won.'

'Really?' Hazel replied.

'This poem is by a Frenchman in French,' Jill replied.

'Really?' Hazel said.

'So there's violence, but it's not funny,' Jill said.

'"Waterloo, Waterloo, Waterloo, morne plaine",' Denise said.

'There you are!' Jill cried.

'What?' Hazel said.

'In French,' Jill said.

'"Morne plaine",' Denise said. "Dismal terrain." After the battle. Wellington declared that there was only one thing worse than a defeat and that was a victory.'

'Do you use informants, Colin?' Denise asked.

'Dad won't talk about that,' Jill said.

'Informants bring info,' Hazel said. 'Dad doesn't.'

'Bed now for you two,' Harpur replied.

And later in bed themselves, Denise said, 'The star of the film, Isabelle Huppert – do you like her kind of looks, Colin?'

'Never seen them,' Harpur said.

'Sort of lovely, high, delicate cheek bones, slim, so elegant, quizzical eyes.'

'I'd probably prefer you.'

'Only probably?'

'*Most* probably. Quizzical eyes might put me off her. I don't like being quizzed. I quiz.'

'In another picture she's a stern music teacher who caves in and sucks a fair-haired boy pupil off near the piano. Musicians in the brass section of an orchestra might talk about their performances as blow jobs, but this was something else.'

'Does the pupil play better afterwards? He'd need to. There's going to be a lot of competition – lads suddenly very keen on practising their scales.'

'How about you?'

'What?'

'Are you better at things afterwards?'

'What things?'

'All of them.'

'I forget,' he replied.

'I think I'll remind you.'

THIRTY-FIVE

'd begun to feel I was doing really well. Of course, I didn't realize at the time that just by being alive I *was* doing really well, so far. I hadn't even heard of Cairn Close at this time, and had only recently met the person who asked me to do a reconnaissance there. That's just a general point. To get to specifics: I'd become full of what I can now see were daft optimism and dafter vanity. Hindsight is something of a speciality for anyone in my situation.

How to explain the optimism and vanity? Well, I think the smart way I'd landed the Righton job years ago gave the right sort of gilded and precocious start: still a school kid, I'd bypassed Rory Mitchell, the Cambridge first, by natural, untaught, brilliant, instinctive flair around supermarket aisles and so on. And then, with a moderate amount of experience in the firm, I'd impressed Bainbridge Williamson enough to be put on the board, Bainbridge no mug, despite his Old Curiosity Shop garb.

Now, with the help of two sweet jailbirds, Enid Aust and, above all, Mrs Lamb, I was apparently going to get into Darien as an authentic, chaperoned emissary – much more useful than simply taking a mid-distance gawp at the house on the day a possibly significant van nosed its way up the gravelled drive and, so it seemed, was rattily turned away. I'd hope to get beyond the cloudiness of 'so it seemed' and 'apparently'. I should collect some genuine, solid stuff.

'Genuine solid stuff' to do with what? Well, to do with *something*, no question. And Jack figured in it some*where*, no question. Clarity might slowly dawn. I would be going to Darien with demands – requests, entreaties – from Jack's mother for him to get out of denial and recognize things as they were. And how *were* things as she saw them? Unsafe. She wanted Jack to get special, close protection – i.e., probably me, though, of course, unarmed: private detectives in Britain don't carry guns. After living in America for so long perhaps she'd forgotten that. She'd probably want to remedy it. But the States was another country. They did things differently there.

I, too, wanted Jack to recognize how things were – unsafe – and to talk to Enid and myself about them; and particularly to myself about them, so I'd know what the hell they were. Surely no decent man could ignore or spurn a loving message from his caring, banged up, markswoman ma, who'd changed her second marriage surname back to his, reaffirming a precious bond.

My thinking was that the visit with Enid to Darien would be an advance, but a small one. The real progress – if I could expect any of this at all – would come via a different house, not Darien. After the call on Jack Lamb I knew I must try to find out what Judith from the very beginning asked me to find out: the role in all this of Failsafe, her brother's place, near Rastelle Major. She'd wanted me to bug a conference room there. I still regarded that as too tricky. Bainbridge had shown me how to bug a parked, empty car, but not how to manage the complexities of wiring up a possibly large room in an occupied, maybe busy, household. The private detective course I'd attended had offered no training in bugging of any kind. As I've said, it was considered. It was considered borderline illegal, and in some cases absolutely and utterly illegal. No respectable training outfit could risk its reputation by giving instruction in those shady skills. But somehow I needed to get more than Judith had told me about Failsafe. That would be difficult. Much more difficult than a threesome chat at Darien. I'd give it some big thought.

There was a practical point. Alice Lamb had said she'd meet Righton's fees for looking after Jack – for looking after Jack as far as it was feasible to look after Jack. If the meeting at Darien revealed a connection with Failsafe I could work officially on that end of the case, covered by his mother's payments, and with Bainbridge Williamson's approval. The dangers that she believed menaced her son might in some way come from Failsafe. 'In some way': another of those convenient, meaningless, evasive jingles. 'So make them clear and concrete, Thomas Wells Hart,' I should have told myself, 'you're big-headed and brassy enough to believe you can.' Early success sometimes brought problems. Confidence could become cockiness, and cockiness could become carelessness. God, I've gone oracular!

I don't know whether this is another slab of hindsight, but I had the feeling even before Jack Lamb opened the door to Enid Aust and me at Darien that the house had something wrong about it, something downcast and even defeated about it. I wouldn't have been able to explain where that notion originated, though. The building had seen some changes over the centuries but was still as handsome and dignified as it had ever been. And Jack, greeting us, sounded, on the face of it, as warm, chirpy and upbeat, as anyone could whose mother was in jail after shooting someone dead on the premises.

Enid had arranged the visit by phone. There were introductions. 'Anyone who comes to me from Ma is extremely welcome,' Jack told her. 'And anyone who comes *with* somebody who comes to me from my mother is also welcome,' he said. He was big and hefty, wearing what seemed to me an army officer's uniform from some foreign country, with two rows of medal ribbons on the chest, several broad golden rank rings on each cuff, and a purple sash worn over one shoulder and fastened to a thick leather midriff belt. His voice echoed in the big, flagstoned hall, the kind of voice that flagstoned halls seemed suitable for, and vice versa.

He led into a large downstairs room, or what I took to have been at some time two separate rooms now knocked into one. Lamb said, 'You can see I'm already acting to some degree on mother's advice. Well, more than advice! Orders! This is normally my gallery, but, look at it now!' The pale-green emulsioned walls were bare. Here and there, I could make out slight patches of discolouration where pictures might have hung for too long. There was a scatter of unoccupied hooks.

It seemed to me that I'd had it right, hadn't I, even before we'd entered Darien: this core area of the house did look appallingly neglected and even abandoned. Without awareness of it, had I developed brilliant powers of intuition, perhaps, in fact, low-level clairvoyance? Now, I felt a kind of guilt at witnessing this miserable come-down. To stare at the sad emptiness and the dismal traces of the scarpered pictures seemed disrespectful and cold. Lamb said, 'I'm keeping everything secure in the strong-room for at least a little while, until I'm feeling more at ease – and until Mother is feeling more at ease.'

'Yes, this is a good start, Jack. I'm sure Alice will be pleased,' Enid said.

'I thought of coming out to tell you last night that I'd done at least part of what she wants,' Lamb said.

Enid looked puzzled. I probably did, too. 'Sorry. "Thought of coming out"?' Enid said.

'To reassure you,' Lamb said.

'Coming out to reassure us where?' Enid replied.

'Well, here, obviously,' Lamb said.

'I don't understand,' I said.

'Nor do I,' Enid said.

'Ah, here's Helen,' Lamb replied.

A girl of about nineteen or twenty came into the gallery carrying a tray with a bottle of champagne on it and four glasses. She moved fluently despite the load, as though she'd had dance training. She wore a long, black, sleeveless singlet with a picture of a lioness facing left on it, light blue shorts, and knee-length woollen socks striped black and white. Her fair hair was streaked with a matching light blue dye. More introductions. 'I told them, Helen, that we'd thought of coming out for a chat last night, perhaps to invite them in for the bubbly.' Lamb said. 'In fact, I think you did step outside briefly, didn't you?'

'Oh, last night! Yes.' She chuckled. 'Jack was serious, but he decided your work must be important and we shouldn't interfere.'

'Work?' Enid said.

'Activity,' Helen replied. 'Important, anyway, whatever we call it.'

We went into another room where there were easy chairs and settees in brown leather, a big stone fireplace and at one end a minstrels' gallery in mahogany. We sat down and Helen poured the wine.

'I think I speak for Tom when I say you have us mystified, Helen, Jack,' Enid said.

'Yes,' I said.

'I don't understand when you talk of coming out to see us,' Enid said.

'Right,' I said.

'Where exactly? What time of day?' Enid asked.

'Night,' Lamb said. 'Have I been tactless? It was supposed to be a secret, was it? And I've barged in regardless.'

'*What* was supposed to be secret?' Enid asked.

'Down near the gate,' Jack said.

'But someone did use a torch briefly, swung it high, apparently checking the gate's usefulness or not as security. So it couldn't be entirely secret,' Helen said.

'Mystery on mystery,' I said.

'We assumed you were doing a bit of a reconnaissance,' Helen replied.

'Of what?' Enid said.

'Inspecting the kind of ground you'd have to patrol night and day if you were to look after Darien and Jack as Alice wants,' Helen said. She went quiet, took a sip of the champagne, gazing over the rim of the flute at Enid. 'But I'm getting the idea – not a very comfortable idea – that Jack and I have made some seriously wrong assumptions.'

'I think you have,' Enid said.

'We weren't out there flashing,' I said.

'Who, then?' Enid said.

'Maybe Ma's anxieties make more sense than I'd thought,' Lamb said. 'We're a target? A target again?'

'Were we idiots?' Helen said. 'This is bad, isn't it?'

'That's how it looks,' Enid replied. 'We've got trouble.'

I liked that – the 'we've'. It meant she'd stick around to help, though the trouble wasn't at all *her* trouble. But she had a grand and tireless loyalty to her chum behind bars, Alice Lamb.

THIRTY-SIX

Now and then when Harpur returned home to Arthur Street his daughters would be entertaining some visitor who wanted to see him and had been persuaded to wait, as had been the case with Mrs Gaston. The girls were good at persuading callers to wait. They had tenacity and a belief in their charming ability to put people at ease, not always true or even half true. But nobody was going to tell the kids of a detective chief superintendent in their own home to fuck off.

On the whole, Harpur disliked these unscheduled meetings. Generally, the visitor brought very private, and possibly dangerous, matter to reveal and discuss. Hazel and Jill would know this, of course, and they'd try to get at what exactly it was by doggedly nosy questioning, especially from Jill – also of course. Harpur realized that in a way he'd set himself up for this kind of situation: his address and telephone number were available in all the directories. Sometimes important information would come because people could get in direct touch without having to go through a police station switchboard and being shunted about between departments. As well as this, though, he thought that anybody who needed the kind of help he could give should be able to reach him unhindered and fast. His daughters approved of this and regarded themselves as part of the news gathering and/or effective, kindly support team. Because of Hazel and Jill, Harpur did wonder occasionally whether it was wise to publish his domestic details. Not many of his colleagues disclosed theirs.

But this evening's visitor could have found his address officially, anyway, by asking at headquarters. 'This lady is to do with art,' Jill said

'Yes, I know her,' Harpur said. 'Pamela Venning. Hello, Pam.'

'Jill and I have been talking to Pamela,' Hazel said. 'Denise is here, but doing some university stuff on her laptop upstairs.'

'Pamela doesn't *like* art, but it's her job all the same,' Jill said, as he took a chair with them in the sitting room. 'She thinks art is unnecessary, that's the point. Pam says art is an insult to whatever the art is about, such as, say, a bowl of fruit, referred to as "still life". Pam considers that if the fruit is there, a real item, why sneak up on it with an easel and steal what it looks like, making it not special any longer and 1 of 1, but now only 1 of 2. Frames, she detests, because they put a sort of boundary or fence around things that shouldn't have a boundary, such as the sea with sailing boats on it, or a puma, not in the zoo, but its right place, the jungle. She believes art is just mankind's way of getting back at Nature for being so strong and free, with cyclones and killer sharks. Mostly she's in London but she goes to other places if there's an art crisis somewhere else. That's us now – somewhere else.'

'Pam's with the arts and antiques outfit at the Met,' Hazel said.

'I needed to speak with you, Colin,' Pamela said.

'Because she wants to talk to you, Dad, it means there must be an art situation here,' Jill said. 'That's the logic of it. And there definitely *was* an art situation when Jack Lamb's mother killed someone up at his big house called Darien – on TV News and in the papers. That was in a private art gallery. There'd be pictures on the walls but they would be there to show what certain things were like, such as the sea or a puma, but the real thing, not in any frame, either, is that pistol knocking a hole in someone and the blood on the gallery floor.'

Hazel said, 'What we wondered was whether an art crisis made you late, Dad, when you went out last night. You said an hour, but, no, much longer. When this difference was mentioned you spoke of complications. You did not explain what complications. Perhaps these were to do with Pamela and art. You did not explain what the complications were, although we would have been quite willing to listen and, in fact, interested.'

'Art is quite a wide topic,' Harpur replied.

'Pam knows Des Iles as well,' Jill said. 'She has known him for years, as a matter of fact, but it's you she's come to see, so it must be something unusual. Many feel it's much easier talking to Dad than to Des Iles, Pamela. Des Iles likes to go off on his own ideas and they're not always to do with what he's supposed to be talking about. He used to come here quite a lot because he fancied Haze, although she was well under age.'

'Slug bitch,' Hazel replied.

'But then he did something pretty good and noble for someone like Des Iles and saved her own-age regular boyfriend, Scott, from running with a drugs gang and its wars – real peril – and after that he left Haze alone. I don't know whether she's pleased or sorry, but I think Dad is pleased. Des had a crimson scarf. He wore it sort of loose, not tucked in, what's known as "swashbuckling".'

'Ulcer,' Hazel replied.

'What I don't understand is how you and Pamela know each other, Dad,' Jill said. 'Pamela told us she worked with Des Iles in London, but you were never in the London police. Haze said you might of been late coming back because it was something to do with Pamela.'

'Might *have* been,' Harpur said.

'You say it might have been, but, if it was, you would *know*. It wouldn't be *might*,' Jill said.

'He was correcting you grammar, again, idiot,' Hazel said. 'Not might *of* been, but might *have* been.'

'So, was the lateness to do with it?' Jill said. 'When he came back late Denise was here. I don't know if you've heard of Denise, but she's really lovely and never asks him why he's been out late, which, if she did, could be to do with jealousy. She trusts him. She lives here quite a lot, but she's a student and has a room in the university buildings called "Jonson Court" without an "h". There's a Johnson *with* an "h" in English Literature who wrote a dictionary and a Jonson without an "h" who wrote plays and called Shakespeare the "sweet swan of Avon". Sometimes Denise sleeps there, and Dad trusts her, too. But when we ask why he was late, it isn't because we think there might be things going on. It's only because we would like to be clear on certain subjects, such as was this when he met you, as a simple yes or no. That would be as a matter of police work, nothing else. Denise is upstairs now, doing an essay or something but when she comes down she wouldn't even think to ask about when you met Dad, because she trusts him and she believes in being very tactful.'

'I think you and Hazel should take her up a cup of tea now
and then you can do one a bit later for Pamela and me, but don't
hurry,' Harpur said.

'Oh, it's like that, is it? Confidential police stuff,' Hazel said.

'I don't know what it is,' Harpur said. 'Pamela hasn't had a
chance to tell me.'

'Yes, it's to do with a development or two,' Pamela said.

'What sort of development?' Jill said.

'Denise won't mind your interrupting her,' Harpur replied.
'She most probably needs a break.'

'It's not what *she* needs, is it, Dad?' Hazel said. 'It's so you
can be private with Pamela.'

'But only because you want to be alone with Pam so you can
talk about certain things that have to be just for the two of you,
isn't it, Dad?' Jill said. 'Things to do with work, not with . . .
with what-you-call.'

'Which what-you-call?' Hazel replied.

'Not what's referred to as "intimate" things.'

'Depends what you mean by "intimate",' Hazel said. 'In any
case, why do these things between them, whatever they are, why
do have to be just for the two of them?'

'Why don't they tell us why they can't tell us?'

'If Dad or Pamela told us why they can't tell us it would be
like telling us what it is they can't tell us,' Jill said.

'So?' Hazel said. 'What about the Freedom of Information
Act?'

'What about it?' Jill said.

'Why haven't we got it?' Hazel said.

'It's only *some* information that's free,' Jill said.

'Who decides which?' Hazel replied.

'Well, Dad or Pam,' Jill said.

'It's not free, then, is it?' Hazel said.

'The bits that are free are free, not the other bits,' Jill said.

'Oh, great,' Hazel said. 'Does she make sense to you, Dad?'

'We'll see you and Denise very shortly,' Harpur replied.

The girls went into the kitchen, Hazel snarling, but quietly.
Pamela said, 'Up to a point they're right.'

'They're often right. Kids – all kids, not just Haze and Jill.
They chew away at things and ask the big daft questions that

turn out not to be so daft. "Except you become like little children." The New Testament had it correct.'

'They see it's strange that I pick you to talk to you, not Des Iles.'

'You'll have your reasons,' Harpur said.

'He tends to take over. That happened several times to me in the Met. If he gets interested in what you tell him he'll say, "Ah, yes, we should obviously handle this thus-wise and thus-wise, I think. You'll agree, I know."'

'Yes, he'll try. He's got the rank to do it. ACC (Ops.). But if he does take over he'll almost always finish whatever it is well, probably better than you or I alone.'

'I know, I know. That's why I don't like it!' she said. 'And then there was the sexual side of things.'

'I didn't know about that.'

'Months. Over now, obviously, but I didn't want to put at risk what was a very good relationship because of disputes about the job. He probably thinks I'd still kowtow. No. I wouldn't like to outright defy him though, even now. Embarrassing. A bit of a tangle,' she said.

'You resented the way he used what you'd told him about, say, an investigation, or tip-off, to get ahead of you?'

'Ah, you understand! And do you deliberately hold stuff back from him sometimes?'

'What is it that troubles you, Pam?' Harpur replied. 'The children and Denise will be here shortly.'

She looked angry for a couple of moments at Harpur's switch of conversation. But then she held up both hands in a surrender signal. 'I'm interested in a house and its inhabitants and visitors – perhaps especially its visitors – over near Rastelle Major. The property's called Failsafe – some kind of *chic* joke, I imagine. The owner is called Keith Vasonne, wife Olive. Neither has any police record. I – we – think that a considerable money laundering business has become centred there based on picture and sculpt trading. It began small and we think with something of a failure. Keith Vasonne, who ran a high-class interior design firm – still does – got persuaded into this more profitable game – we're talking millions, Colin, if not billions. Apparently, he tried something for one of these new type clients on that dodgy art dealer,

Jack Lamb, whose house on your ground we were looking at the other night. Darien.'

'Yes, of course,' Harpur said. 'The house is named after something in a poem.'

'Possibly. But although this attempt at swapping tainted cash for some of Lamb's collection didn't come off, several of Vasonne's new contacts liked the idea of working laundering activities through a nice, detached provincial suburban villa with a cooperative owner, and decided things would be organized very well through Failsafe. Lamb's refusal didn't seem relevant any longer. We think the business is becoming, or has become already, nationwide, and possible Euro, dollar, yen and rouble wide. Big money comes to Failsafe, and classical pictures come, too, and leave with their new culture-seeking, crooked, kidnappers, crack merchants, protection providers, people traders. There can be a lot of money – and I mean cash – there can be a lot of it and a lot of high value art, probably genuine, in that house at any time. We think the operation is run by a woman, Charlotte Ruth Medim, aged twenty-nine of Hampstead, London. She might have taken part in the original attempt at a negotiated deal with Lamb. Keith Vasonne made the actual failed contact, but she oversaw the arrangements.'

Harpur said . . .

But why always Harpur?

THIRTY-SEVEN

Let me have a word, OK? I think I had a rickety conversation with this Charlotte Ruth Medim in a layby not far from Darien. She drove an Audi.

THIRTY-EIGHT

Pamela said, 'Medim and her associates are naturally very security conscious. At some periods the house is stuffed with this enormous wealth – lucre and/or art trove. She and her people employ four heavies, probably armed, to do sentry shifts covering all day and all night. Obviously, we want to move against Failsafe when the potential catch is at its maximum: people and treasure. That will entail neutralizing the guards somehow. It's under discussion. Why I've come to talk to you, Colin, is that because of the inevitable busyness and comings and goings at the house a neighbourhood cop or simply neighbours might begin to wonder what was happening. And they might try to find out.

'The neighbourhood cop, for instance, might report the activity to his sergeant, who might refer it to his inspector, and might refer it to you. And you might decide to organize some inquiries. The inquiries could turn out to be worth taking further – might, in fact, lead to a raid. But it would probably be a premature raid. That is, the timing might not be right for the best, the full, result. So, I'm here, Colin, to ask that if you get a report of that kind you don't rush to act. When we are ready, we would, of course, notify you and Desmond and would need your assistance. But we'd like to have control of the timetable.'

'I've read about something like this, haven't I?' Harpur said.

'Have you?'

'Boston in America. There's a book about it called *Black Mass*. The local police wanted to move against a known gangster. The FBI objected because they required delays to suit other plans they had, needing the help of the local villain.'

'The Whitey Bulger case,' she said. 'Yes, something like that.'

'Here's Denise,' Jill said, leading her and Hazel into the sitting room. 'She recently went to see a French film called *Tip Top*.'

Jill had made some more tea and the three of them began to discuss films generally. Harpur wasn't much use at this. He would have liked to tell Pamela that he thought it a bit of bloody cheek to come in on their ground and start a private investigation, even if she had shagged Iles a while ago. But because of the children and Denise he'd stay quiet on that topic now. And on *their* topic, the cinema, because he didn't have anything to say. Or nothing to say except about *Fargo* on one of the movie channels, and this would probably seem like very old history to them.

THIRTY-NINE

Enid said, 'I'm going to hang on in this area for a while longer, Tom, in case you get somewhere with Alice's request for you to do anything more to protect Jack.'

'Right,' I said. 'I'm going to try to find what I can at the Failsafe house. Perhaps I should have had a go at that much earlier.'

'I'm in an hotel, The Raven,' she said.

'Is it OK?'

'It's OK, but not for me now. I feel conspicuous there. I've signed in. Don't like doing that. Makes me traceable,' she said.

'That bad?'

'I had a little trouble back home, you know. Why I was in with Alice.'

'What kind of trouble?'

'Trouble. Some people are annoyed still. They're thinking vengeance.'

'Vengeance for what?'

'I'd like to get somewhere more anonymous. I've seen a flat advertised in this end of the city. I wonder if you could go and have a look at it, Tom. See with your private eye skills whether I'd be safe there?'

'Safe from what? Whom? What did you do?'

'Could you, please?'

'Where is it?'

'It's called Cairn Close.'

FORTY

Although Desmond Iles sometimes became unruly at funerals and might have to be suppressed by Harpur, the assistant chief disapproved of violence by any others at the service itself or the wake following, especially fighting by women. Iles had told Harpur that he considered there was 'something uncultured and even sickening about seeing and hearing a woman flattened after a punch or punches from anyone, male or female, 'but surely it is most distressing if the punch or punches came from another woman.' He saw a kind of social collapse typified in such an incident. He reckoned there was a uniquely awful sound when a woman hit the ground like that, possibly unconscious. It was made up of the impact noise of upper body bones such as the chin, shoulder, head hitting the floor, plus bling, shins and knees.

At the pub buffet after Thomas Wells Hart's funeral, Harpur and Iles spoke for quite some while to Hart's family, girlfriend and colleagues, but Harpur felt that throughout the conversations with this group of half a dozen or so the assistant chief watched, off and on, all sections of the room. The party took place in the changing quarters of a community sports centre and was non-alcoholic. Harpur picked up an odour of resin.

Iles said, 'Naturally, I don't in the least understand how your boy chances to get shot to pieces in a fairly decent suburb, Mr and Mrs Hart. Harpur probably knows and will, I'm sure, tell you the lot, if only to make me look a right hopeless slob. I'm used to that kind of insolence from him, but it will come as a shock to you, and I'm sorry.'

Harpur said, 'We think—'

'Which "we" is that, then, Harpur? Does it include me? I only happen to be the assistant chief constable in charge of operations. Does that entitle me to be included in your term "we"?'

'We think,' Harpur replied, 'that as part of his work as a private investigator he went to look at a house over towards Rastelle

Major which he suspected was used as headquarters of a money laundering outfit. We now know he was correct and our colleague, Pamela Venning with a contingent of local and London officers have closed that down and made arrests, though we are still seeking the gunman or gunmen who killed Thomas. Perhaps he poked about there too insistently and got spotted and followed. He was himself an expert tracker, but, unfortunately that doesn't necessarily mean he'd notice a motorized stalker or stalkers on his own tail.'

Judith Vasonne, standing alone with a brown-bread sandwich in her hand and near enough to overhear, said, 'I told him about the house a long while ago, urged him to investigate. I don't believe he gave much weight to that suggestion. I think he felt it was a duty to do a thorough visit now, to make up for delaying. Oh, God, I feel responsible for his death.'

'So you should,' Daphne Davenpole said, joining them. She wasn't eating or drinking.

'Why do you say that?' Hart's father said.

'Because she is and was a cruel, unbalanced bitch,' Judith said. Iles, that vigilant, part-time, pacifier, moved slightly with his turkey leg, so that he stood between Vasonne and Davenpole, making sure there were none of those gender tainted punches he found so revolting.

Although Iles saw himself as an impassioned fan and observer of connections and links, there were obviously times when he recognized that some people should be kept apart.

He could be a great amalgamator, he could be an exquisite portcullis.